倍斯特出版事業有限公司
Best Publishing Ltd.

一次就考到

雅思
說聽讀
6.5+

倍斯特編輯部 ◎ 著

運用「影子跟讀法」，
雙管齊下練「聽」、「說」，打好口譯基礎

MP3

4大高分關鍵

❶ 熟悉「聽」聽力短句
▶ 規劃「短句」跟讀練習，「用力聽」且即刻適應聽力節奏，在section 1&2 得分關鍵中不失分。

❷ 聽懂學術場景長句
▶ 特別設計「長句」跟讀練習，在section 3&4不因聽力訊息較長，而影響聽力得分。

❸ 練就短逐步口譯能力
▶ 收錄34組「長對話」跟讀練習，隨著聽力訊息停留在腦海的時間加長，逐步養成篩選訊息重點的能力，分辨較重要和次要訊息的差異，並針對題目做出準確的判斷。

❹ 無壓力下練習口說
▶ 精選最夯生活話題，從單句漸進到段落描述，分享完自身經驗也完成答題。

Editor's 編者序 Preface

在聽力考試中許多人其實誤解了聽力測驗的目的，就如同報考指定科目考試一樣，許多人寫了歷屆試題、上了補習班、檢討了試題內容或不斷複習，卻未能於實際考試中考取滿分，歸根究底在於：寫試題只是熟悉考試方式和提升臨場反應。寫試題只是檢測當下寫該份試卷時，所反應出的成績，若本身對學科如數學科等，某些單元的理解上沒有提升的話，是不可能獲取高分的。

英文聽力也是如此，許多人常犯了本末倒置的學習錯誤，認為寫了劍橋雅思真題等模擬題加上反覆檢討，就能於實際考試中獲取一定的分數，但卻總是事與願違。因為考生本身的聽力理解力並未因為寫了幾份試題就有所提升。此外，聽力專注力也影響著聽力成績的高低，就如同聽力良好的學習者，若是分心了，也極可能拿到與聽力稍差者同等的聽力分數。

有鑑於此，編輯部於本書聽力篇規劃了三個部分，分別是聽力講解篇、聽力演練篇、聽力實戰篇，是藉由口譯中的 shadowing（跟讀）等搭配短對話、短段落和長對話作練習，幫助考生提升本身聽英文時的專注力；但須注意的是，每個人程度不同，書中只提供部分練習引導讀者練習聽力，

實際上讀者仍需藉由歐美影集或劍橋雅思真題音檔（建議 7－11）作大量的 shadowing 的練習，才能於應考時獲取理想成績。

在口說篇則規劃了跳脫模板式的學習，一來背模板或範文效用不高，考官閱人無數，能從回答中了解是否是背誦的答案，實際上考生只需將自身經驗融入雅思口說考試即可，且這方法也能於考試中避免因緊張而忘記所背誦的答案是什麼，造成語句不連貫而停頓等尷尬情況。

書中教你由單句口說為開頭，練習 30 個常見的生活主題，由這些主題，演練短敘述（即「一氣呵成」單元），並於短敘述後融入自身答案，改成自身經驗的回答，將自己旅遊等體驗融入回答，在答題上更貼切、逼真，畢竟人與人之間交談是種互動，要讓考官覺得是一對一的對談，而不是你來參加「考試」，相信藉由這些主題練習後，在應考雅思口說上能更切中考試核心更充分的應戰。

編輯部敬上

Instructions

使用說明

❶ 初步説明「**聽力講解篇**」概念。

❷ 由每個「**關鍵句**」作聽力練習,關鍵句下方有「**字彙輔助**」。

❸ 每個關鍵句最下方均有「**小提點**」,清楚了解訓練聽力的方式。

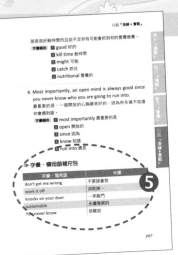

❹ 由「**單句口說**」開始作口說練習，每個例句下方均有「**字彙輔助**」。

❺ 每個單元均有「**字彙、慣用語補充包**」，特別收錄道地慣用語，用於口說考試中更無往不利。

❻ 在數組的單句口說練習後，逐步練就「**一氣呵成**」的功力，能以英語對特定主題進行描述。

❼ 每個單元均規劃「**你來試試看**」，不死背答案，而是融入自己的經驗並用於實際考試中。

CONTENTS 目次

Part 1 雅思聽力篇

Part 2 雅思口說篇

口說『演練+實戰』

Part **1**
雅思聽力篇

篇章概述

雅思聽力篇包含了講解、演練和實戰篇，先由講解篇學會如何以 shadowing 練習短對話，再以演練篇練習長句的 shadowing 練習，最後做長篇對話的 shadowing 練習。逐步打好英聽根基才是王道，專注力跟聽力理解力沒提升，做題目只會浪費時間，快點動手練習吧！

（小提點：別忘了做完此篇後，在掌握大概的學習技巧後，記得把劍橋雅思 7-11 音檔拿來做 shadowing 練習吧！）

UNIT 1 ▶▶ Specialty Food 美味名產

▶▶ 聽力講解

　　此篇為「聽力講解篇」，相信讀者能大致了解 shadowing 的功用並且逐步邁向聽力的下一步，即聽數句對話內容，然後作 shadowing 的練習，此章節規劃了由聽單句的 shadowing 練習到聽連續 6 句並作 shadowing 的練習，從中調整自己聽英文的腳步，並在此章節紮好英文聽力基礎，注意自己聽力專注力，為下個章節即聽力演練篇作好準備，也能在實際雅思聽力的長對話、學術場景的聽力中奠定好基礎，現在就一起動身，開始由聽「**短對話**」開始！

※因每個讀者程度不同，若是稍具程度的讀者，可以跳過此章節喔！直接由下個篇章開始，直接作長句的 shadowing 練習喔！

▶▶ 單句 shadowing 練習 MP3 01

※現在請跟著 CD 覆誦，練習單句 shadowing 練習，第一次先跟著 CD 以相同速度覆誦，第二次跟第三次後可以隨個人程度調整並於聽到句子內容後，拉長數秒或更長時間作練習。

KEY 1

I just threw up a little in my mouth!
我想到就想吐！

字彙輔助　1 throw up 吐

　　　　　　2 in my mouth 在嘴裡

小提點　第二次練習時，可以等 CD 播放到 up 這個介系詞再開始跟讀，也可以隨著更熟練後，將跟讀時間漸漸往後至 CD 播放到 my 後再跟著讀，最後漸漸強化到整個句子唸完後再完整覆誦一整句。

KEY 2

I would probably sue them about abusing animals or potentially poisoning the visitors.

我應該會告他們虐待動物或是意圖讓他們的遊客中毒。

字彙輔助　1 sue 控告

　　　　　　2 potentially 潛在地

小提點　第二次練習時，可以等 CD 播放到 them 這個單字再開始跟讀，也可以隨著更熟練後，將跟讀時間漸漸往後至 CD 播放到 poisoning 後再跟著讀，最後漸漸強化到整個句子唸完後再完整覆誦一整句。

KEY 3

I hope they have very good reasons not because they have great proteins.

我希望他們吃這些東西的原因不只是因為有豐富的蛋白質。

字彙輔助 ❶ reason 理由
❷ protein 蛋白質

小提點 第二次練習時，可以等 CD 播放到 very 這個單字再開始跟讀，也可以隨著更熟練後，將跟讀時間漸漸往後至 CD 播放到 have 後再跟著讀，最後漸漸強化到整個句子唸完後再完整覆誦一整句。

KEY **4**

I'm all acted up just by thinking about it.
我光用想的就氣起來了。

字彙輔助 ❶ act up 動氣、出毛病、調皮
❷ think about 想起來

小提點 第二次練習時，可以等 CD 播放到 acted 這個單字再開始跟讀，也可以隨著更熟練後，將跟讀時間漸漸往後至 CD 播放到 thinking 後再跟著讀，最後漸漸強化到整個句子唸完後再完整覆誦一整句。

KEY **5**

I'm intimidated, but I would probably give it a shot.
我會怕，可是我覺得我應該會試試看。

聽力『講解』

聽力『演練』

聽力『實戰』

口說『演練+實戰』

字彙輔助　① intimidate 威脅
　　　　　　② give it a shot 嘗試看看

小提點　　第二次練習時，可以等 CD 播放到 intimidated 這個單字再開始跟讀，也可以隨著更熟練後，將跟讀時間漸漸往後至 CD 播放到 give 後再跟著讀，最後漸漸強化到整個句子唸完後再完整覆誦一整句。

KEY 6

I mean as long as I'm not doing something illegal.
我的意思是說，反正只要是不違法。

字彙輔助　① as long as 只要
　　　　　　② illegal 不合法的

小提點　　第二次練習時，可以等 CD 播放到 I'm 這邊再開始跟讀，也可以隨著更熟練後，將跟讀時間漸漸往後至 CD 播放到 something 後再跟著讀，最後漸漸強化到整個句子唸完後再完整覆誦一整句。

UNIT 2 ▶▶ Specialty Food 美味名產

▶▶ 聽力講解

　　此篇為「聽力講解篇」，相信讀者能大致了解 shadowing 的功用並且逐步邁向聽力的下一步，即聽數句對話內容，然後作 shadowing 的練習，此章節規劃了由聽單句的 shadowing 練習到聽連續 6 句並作 shadowing 的練習，從中調整自己聽英文的腳步，並在此章節紮好英文聽力基礎，注意自己聽力專注力，為下個章節即聽力演練篇作好準備，也能在實際雅思聽力的長對話、學術場景的聽力中奠定好基礎，現在就一起動身，開始由聽「**短對話**」開始！

※因每個讀者程度不同，若是稍具程度的讀者，可以跳過此章節喔！直接由下個篇章開始，直接作長對話的 shadowing 練習喔！

▶▶ 雙句 shadowing 練習 `MP3 02`

※現在請跟著 CD 覆誦，練習 2 句 shadowing 練習，第一次先跟著 CD 以相同速度覆誦，第二次跟第三次後可以隨個人程度調整並於聽到句子內容後，拉長數秒或更長時間作練習。

KEY **1**

I was a bit skeptical at the beginning because it was basically raw ham with melon, but when I tried it, it was the perfect marriage of the foods.

起初我很懷疑這個生火腿跟香瓜的組合，可是我一吃就發現這個組合真是太完美了。

字彙輔助　① skeptical 懷疑的
　　　　　　② marriage 組合

小提點　這個句子較長，可於第二次練習時，等 CD 播放到 because 這個單字再開始跟讀，也可以隨著更熟練後，將跟讀時間漸漸往後至 CD 播放到 melon 或更之後的單字 perfect 後再跟著讀，最後漸漸強化到整個句子唸完後再完整覆誦一整句。

KEY **2**

This appetizer is definitely the embodiment of "Less is more." I tried it in a couple of restaurants here, but it just wasn't quite the same.

這個開胃菜真的是實踐「少就是多」。我有在這裡的幾家餐廳點這個，可是就是跟在義大利吃到的不太一樣。

字彙輔助　① appetizer 開胃菜
　　　　　　② the same 相同的

小提點 第二次練習時，可以等 CD 播放到 embodiment 這個單字再開始跟讀，也可以隨著更熟練後，將跟讀時間漸漸往後至 CD 播放到 restaurants 後再跟著讀，最後漸漸強化到整個句子唸完後再完整覆誦一整句。

KEY 3

I would definitely go back to Spain for their Paella. It has everything I love.

我一定會回去西班牙吃他們的西班牙海鮮燉飯。那燉飯裡面有我所愛的每樣食物。

字彙輔助 1 definitely 一定
2 Paella 海鮮燉飯

小提點 第二次練習時，可以等 CD 播放到 Spain 這個單字再開始跟讀，也可以隨著更熟練後，將跟讀時間漸漸往後至 CD 播放到 everything 後再跟著讀，最後漸漸強化到整個句子唸完後再完整覆誦一整句。

KEY 4

I even knew I was going to love it when I saw it. The smell was just impossible to resist.

當一開始光看到那道菜，我就知道我會超愛這道菜的。那道菜的味道是無法抗拒的。

字彙輔助　1 love 喜愛
　　　　　　 2 resist 抵擋

小提點　第二次練習時，可以等 CD 播放到 saw 這個單字再開始跟讀，也可以隨著更熟練後，將跟讀時間漸漸往後至 CD 播放到 impossible 後再跟著讀，最後漸漸強化到整個句子唸完後再完整覆誦一整句。

KEY 5

I would want to go back to Australia for their meat pies. I love how the Aussies make their pies savory.
我會想要回澳洲吃他們的肉派。我很喜歡澳洲人把他們的派做成鹹的！

字彙輔助　1 Australia 澳洲
　　　　　　 2 savory 鹹的

小提點　第二次練習時，可以等 CD 播放到 meat 這個單字再開始跟讀，也可以隨著更熟練後，將跟讀時間漸漸往後至 CD 播放到 Aussies 後再跟著讀，最後漸漸強化到整個句子唸完後再完整覆誦一整句。

UNIT 3 ▶▶ Specialty Food 美味名產

▶▶ 聽力講解

　　此篇為「聽力講解篇」，相信讀者能大致了解 shadowing 的功用並且逐步邁向聽力的下一步，即聽數句對話內容，然後作 shadowing 的練習，此章節規劃了由聽單句的 shadowing 練習到聽連續 6 句並作 shadowing 的練習，從中調整自己聽英文的腳步，並在此章節紮好英文聽力基礎，注意自己聽力專注力，為下個章節即聽力演練篇作好準備，也能在實際雅思聽力的長對話、學術場景的聽力中奠定好基礎，現在就一起動身，開始由聽「**短對話**」開始！

※因每個讀者程度不同，若是稍具程度的讀者，可以跳過此章節喔！直接由下個篇章開始，直接作長對話的 shadowing 練習喔！

▶▶ 3 句 shaowing 練習 MP3 03

※現在請跟著 CD 覆誦，練習 3 句 shadowing 練習，第一次先跟著 CD 以相同速度覆誦，第二次跟第三次後可以隨個人程度調整並於聽到句子內容後，拉長數秒或更長時間作練習。

KEY 1

Puffer fish sashimi in Japan was the scariest thing I've ever tried. I can literally say that I risked my life trying this dish. Sweat was coming out from my palms when I knew that there was still a very small chance for me to get seriously poisoned eating this dish.

我在日本吃的河豚生魚片是至今我吃過最恐怖的東西。真的可以說是冒著生命危險吃了這道菜。當我知道還是有很些微的機會會嚴重中毒的時候，我的手心開始冒汗。

字彙輔助

1 puffer 河豚

2 sashimi 生魚片

3 scariest 最恐怖的

4 seriously poisoned 嚴重中毒

小提點 此單元句子拓展為 3 句，可於第二次練習時，等 CD 播放到某個單字再開始跟讀，也可以隨著更熟練後，分次將跟讀時間往後至 CD 播放到第一句結束、第二句結束後再跟著讀，最後漸漸強化到 3 個句子唸完後再開始覆誦全部句子。

KEY **2**

Normally, I wouldn't do that, but I just really wanted to challenge myself on this one. So that I can tell you that I've tried it. It wasn't too cheap, but the meat tasted really pure and clean.

正常來說我不會想吃，可是我真的很想挑戰這個，所以現在我可以跟你說我試過了。它其實沒有很便宜，但是肉質真的很純淨和乾淨。

字彙輔助 1 challenge 挑戰

小提點 此單元句子拓展為 **3** 句，可於第二次練習時，等 CD 播放到某個單字再開始跟讀，也可以隨著更熟練後，分次將跟讀時間往後至 CD 播放到第一句結束、第二句結束後再跟著讀，最後漸漸強化到 **3** 個句子唸完後再開始覆誦全部句子。

KEY **3**

Have you heard of "balut" before? It's the developing duck embryo people eat in Southeast Asia. Yep, it's a boiled egg with an actual developing duckling inside.

你之前有聽過"鴨仔蛋"嗎？它就是東南亞人會吃的正在發育中的鴨胚胎蛋。對的，就是水煮蛋裡面有一隻正在發育中的真的小鴨子。

字彙輔助 1 balut 鴨仔蛋
　　　　　 2 developing 正在發育中的

3 embryo 胚胎

4 Southeast Asia 東南亞

小提點　此單元句子拓展為 3 句，可於第二次練習時，等 CD 播放到某個單字再開始跟讀，也可以隨著更熟練後，分次將跟讀時間往後至 CD 播放到第一句結束、第二句結束後再跟著讀，最後漸漸強化到 3 個句子唸完後再開始覆誦全部句子。

KEY 4

The first time I saw it by the street in Vietnam, I thought they just accidentally picked the wrong egg! Little did I know that they chose the ones with the ducklings inside on purpose! I had to try it just for the sake of it.

我第一次在越南的路邊看到的時候，還以為他們是不小心選錯蛋了，結果後來才知道他們就是故意要選裡面有小鴨子的！就是看在這麼奇怪的份上，我當時一定要吃一下。

字彙輔助　1 Vietnam 越南

2 accidentally 意外地

小提點　此單元句子拓展為 3 句，可於第二次練習時，等 CD 播放到某個單字再開始跟讀，也可以隨著更熟練後，分次將跟讀時間往後至 CD 播放到第一句結束、第二句結束後再跟著讀，最後漸漸強化到 3 個句子唸完後再開始覆誦全部句子。

UNIT 4 ▶▶ Shopping 購物

▶▶ 聽力講解

　　此篇為「聽力講解篇」，相信讀者能大致了解 shadowing 的功用並且逐步邁向聽力的下一步，即聽數句對話內容，然後作 shadowing 的練習，此章節規劃了由聽單句的 shadowing 練習到聽連續 6 句並作 shadowing 的練習，從中調整自己聽英文的腳步，並在此章節紮好英文聽力基礎，注意自己聽力專注力，為下個章節即聽力演練篇作好準備，也能在實際雅思聽力的長對話、學術場景的聽力中奠定好基礎，現在就一起動身，開始由聽「**短對話**」開始！

※因每個讀者程度不同，若是稍具程度的讀者，可以跳過此章節喔！直接由下個篇章開始，直接作長對話的 shadowing 練習喔！

▶▶ 4 句 shaowing 練習 MP3 04

※現在請跟著 CD 覆誦，練習 3 句 shadowing 練習，第一次先跟著 CD 以相同速度覆誦，第二次跟第三次後可以隨個人程度調整並於聽到句子內容後，拉長數秒或更長時間作練習。

KEY 1

Am I a mall person? Excuse me, I can live in a mall. Of course, I am a mall person, and I'm not shameful about it at all. I love everything about shopping in a mall.

我喜歡購物中心嗎？不好意思，我還可以住在購物中心裡。我當然喜歡購物囉，而且我一點也不害羞。我喜歡購物中心的每一件事。

字彙輔助 ① mall 購物中心

小提點 此單元句子拓展為 4 句，可於第二次練習時，等 CD 播放到某個單字再開始跟讀，也可以隨著更熟練後，分次將跟讀時間往後至 CD 播放到第一句結束、第二句結束、第三句結束後再跟著讀，最後漸漸強化到 4 個句子唸完後再開始覆誦全部句子。

KEY 2

You get your nails done, you take home beautiful clothes, and you can sit down at the food court to eat or get a cup of gourmet coffee. There is just so much to see and try on. It is a stress-relief process for me really.

你可以做指甲，帶漂亮的衣服回家，你還可以在美食街吃東西或喝杯高級的咖啡。在購物中心裡有好多東西可以看跟試穿。對我來說其實真的是一個紓壓的方式。

27

字彙輔助　1 nail 指甲
2 beautiful 美麗的
3 food court 美食街
4 stress-relief 紓壓

小提點　此單元句子拓展為 4 句，可於第二次練習時，等 CD 播放到某個單字再開始跟讀，也可以隨著更熟練後，分次將跟讀時間往後至 CD 播放到第一句結束、第二句結束、第三句結束後再跟著讀，最後漸漸強化到 4 個句子唸完後再開始覆誦全部句子。

KEY 3

No, not even a tiny bit. I guess I just don't find material things attractive. Nevertheless, I do have a thing for the sporting goods. I guess I don't like shopping, but I do need to get necessities. Yep, that's what I'm trying to say.

不，一點都不是。物質的東西就真的一點都不吸引我。儘管如此，運動用品對我來說是我的死穴。我想可能是因為我不喜歡購物，但是我還是得買一些必需品啦。嗯，沒錯，我的意思就是那樣。

字彙輔助　1 tiny 微小的
2 material 物質的
3 attractive 吸引人的
4 have a thing for 死穴
5 necessity 必需品

小提點　此單元句子拓展為 4 句，可於第二次練習時，等 CD 播放到某個單字再開始跟讀，也可以隨著更熟練後，分次將跟讀時間往後至 CD 播放到第一句結束、第二句結束、第三句結束後再跟著讀，最後漸漸強化到 4 個句子唸完後再開始覆誦全部句子。

KEY 4

I don't mind digging out all the goodies even if it means it'll take hours. It's the result that counts. I often find goods that are way under their original prices. It's amazing how much discount you can get sometimes.

我不介意挖好貨，即使要花上好幾個小時也沒關係。結果最重要。我常找到很多東西是比原價便宜超多的東西，有時候你得到的折扣會讓你大吃一驚。

字彙輔助
1 dig out 挖掘出、找出
2 goodies 好貨
3 result 結果
4 original 原始的
5 discount 折扣

小提點　此單元句子拓展為 4 句，可於第二次練習時，等 CD 播放到某個單字再開始跟讀，也可以隨著更熟練後，分次將跟讀時間往後至 CD 播放到第一句結束、第二句結束、第三句結束後再跟著讀，最後漸漸強化到 4 個句子唸完後再完開始覆誦全部句子。

UNIT 5 ▶▶ Shopping 購物

▶▶ 聽力講解

　　此篇為「聽力講解篇」，相信讀者能大致了解 shadowing 的功用並且逐步邁向聽力的下一步，即聽數句對話內容，然後作 shadowing 的練習，此章節規劃了由聽單句的 shadowing 練習到聽連續 6 句並作 shadowing 的練習，從中調整自己聽英文的腳步，並在此章節紮好英文聽力基礎，注意自己聽力專注力，為下個章節即聽力演練篇作好準備，也能在實際雅思聽力的長對話、學術場景的聽力中奠定好基礎，現在就一起動身，開始由聽「**短對話**」開始！

※因每個讀者程度不同，若是稍具程度的讀者，可以跳過此章節喔！直接由下個篇章開始，直接作長對話的 shadowing 練習喔！

▶▶ 5 句 shaowing 練習 MP3 05

※現在請跟著 CD 覆誦，練習 5 句 shadowing 練習，第一次先跟著 CD 以相同速度覆誦，第二次跟第三次後可以隨個人程度調整並於聽到句子內容後，拉長數秒或更長時間作練習。

KEY 1

I would never bargain. How can you possibly bargain in a mall? It's so not classy. I don't care about one or two more dollars really, and it's just awkward begging for a lower price. I don't know how people can do it.

我一定不會殺價的。你怎麼可能會在購物中心裡殺價？一點都不優雅。我真的不在意多了一塊還是兩塊，真的，而且要拜託他們把價格壓更低就是一件蠻尷尬的事。我不懂怎麼有人可以做到。

字彙輔助

1 possibly 可能地
2 mall 購物中心
3 care about 在意
4 dollar 元
5 awkward 笨拙的
6 beg 乞求
7 lower 較低的

小提點 此單元句子拓展為 5 句，可於第二次練習時，等 CD 播放到某個單字再開始跟讀，也可以隨著更熟練後，分次將跟讀時間往後至 CD 播放到第一句結束、第二句結束、第三句結束、第四句結束後再跟著讀，最後漸漸強化到 5 個句子唸完後再開始覆誦全部句子。

KEY 2

I don't really have one, but I am mostly just honest about it. I'll say something like " It's a little out of my budget, but I would love to get this from you. Do you think we can work something out here?" And it works really well sometimes. Just be sincere I guess.

我沒有什麼殺手鐧耶，不過我通常就是很誠實。我會説：「這個有點超出我的預算，但是我真的很想跟你買。你有什麼好的辦法嗎？」這樣説有的時候真的很管用。我想就是要很誠懇吧。

字彙輔助
1 mostly 大部分地
2 honest 誠實的
3 budget 預算
4 out of my budget 超出我的預算
5 work something out 想出……解決辦法
6 work 有用、達到……效果
7 sincere 誠懇的

小提點 此單元句子拓展為 5 句，可於第二次練習時，等 CD 播放到某個單字再開始跟讀，也可以隨著更熟練後，分次將跟讀時間往後至 CD 播放到第一句結束、第二句結束、第三句結束、第四句結束後再跟著讀，最後漸漸強化到 5 個句子唸完後再開始覆誦全部句子。

KEY 3

I'll say something like if it's xxx dollars, then I'll get it. Of course, you can't go crazy low. I always shop around and compare the prices first, and then give a reasonable price. If you do your homework, you usually get what you want with the price you like even more! Although sometimes I'll say it's my birthday...

我會說「如果是……元的話，我就買了！」不過當然你不能殺太低。我總是都是先到處逛逛然後比較價錢，最後再給了一個合理的價格。如果你有做好功課的話，你通常會買到你喜歡的東西，而且是用令你滿意的價錢買到的。不過有的時候我會說今天是我的生日…

字彙輔助

1 crazy 瘋狂的

2 shop 購物

3 compare 比較

4 price 價格

5 reasonable 合理的

6 sometimes 有時候

7 birthday 生日

小提點 此單元句子拓展為 5 句，可於第二次練習時，等 CD 播放到某個單字再開始跟讀，也可以隨著更熟練後，分次將跟讀時間往後至 CD 播放到第一句結束、第二句結束、第三句結束、第四句結束後再跟著讀，最後漸漸強化到 5 個句子唸完後再開始覆誦全部句子。

UNIT 6 ▶▶ Shopping 購物

▶▶ 聽力講解

　　此篇為「聽力講解篇」，相信讀者能大致了解 shadowing 的功用並且逐步邁向聽力的下一步，即聽數句對話內容，然後作 shadowing 的練習，此章節規劃了由聽單句的 shadowing 練習到聽連續 6 句並作 shadowing 的練習，從中調整自己聽英文的腳步，並在此章節絭好英文聽力基礎，注意自己聽力專注力，為下個章節即聽力實戰篇作好準備，也能在實際雅思聽力的長對話、學術場景的聽力中奠定好基礎，現在就一起動身，開始由聽「**短對話**」開始！

※因每個讀者程度不同，若是稍具程度的讀者，可以跳過此章節喔！直接由下個篇章開始，直接作長對話的 shadowing 練習喔！

▶▶ 6 句 shaowing 練習 MP3 06

※現在請跟著 CD 覆誦，練習 5 句 shadowing 練習，第一次先跟著 CD 以相同速度覆誦，第二次跟第三次後可以隨個人程度調整並於聽到句子內容後，拉長數秒或更長時間作練習。

KEY 1

I like to get things that are made from that place. It just brings back the memories when I see the things I get from those places... Alright... and it's easier for me to remember where I went. It's the true purpose of a souvenir! And I also feel like I can blend in when I'm wearing the stuffs that are made by the local designers there.

我喜歡買的是從那個地方製造的東西。當我看到那些東西就會帶回我在那裡的時候的回憶……好啦，而且對我來說也比較容易記得我去了哪裡。那就是紀念品真正的目的啊！而且在那裡的時候穿當地設計師做的東西也讓我覺得我比較融入當地！

字彙輔助

1 are made from 製造

2 bring back 帶回

3 memory 記憶、回憶

4 remember 記住

5 purpose 目的

6 souvenir 紀念品

7 blend in 融入

8 local 當地的

9 designer 設計師

小提點 此單元句子拓展為 6 句，可於第二次練習時，等 CD 播放到某個單字再開始跟讀，也可以隨著更熟練後，分次將跟讀時間往後至 CD 播放到第一句結束、第二句結束、第三句結束、第四句結束、第五句結束後再跟著讀，最後漸漸強化到 6 個句子唸完後再開始覆誦全部句子。

KEY 2

Like I said, I don't really shop that much at all. However, I like to collect the travel destination magnets when I'm traveling. I always look for a cool one when I'm traveling. I've already had an awesome collection at home. I think I'll need to get a bigger refrigerator next. Hahaha...

就像我剛剛說的，我真的不太喜歡買東西。但是，我旅行的時候喜歡收集旅遊景點的磁鐵。我每次旅行的時候都在找一些酷的磁鐵。我在家裡已經有一些很棒的收集。我想我下個要買的東西應該就是一個大一點的冰箱了！哈哈哈……

字彙輔助　1 like I said 就像我剛剛說的

2 shop 購物、逛商店

3 collect 收集、收藏

4 destination 目的地

5 magnet 磁鐵

6 awesome 很棒的、令人驚嘆的

7 collection 收藏

8 refrigerator 冰箱

小提點　此單元句子拓展為 6 句，可於第二次練習時，等 CD 播放到某個單字再開始跟讀，也可以隨著更熟練後，分次將跟讀時間往後至 CD 播放到第一句結束、第二句結束、第三句結束、第四句結束、第五句結束後再跟著讀，最後漸漸強化到 6 個句子唸完後再開始覆誦全部句子。

KEY 3

I usually just go with the flow and take a chance. You never know whom you are going to meet and what you might get into. That's why I never make any reservation when I'm going to the restaurants. Most of the time, I meet people and they usually have something in mind. Other times, I just go to any restaurant that I think it is interesting. I found many cool little places this way.

我通常就是跟著感覺走耶，然後就冒個險。你永遠不知道你會遇到誰或是會遇到什麼事。這也就是為什麼如果我要去餐廳吃飯的話，我從來都不訂位。大部分的時候，我遇到的人都會有想要去的地方。其他的時候，我就去我覺得蠻有趣的餐廳看看。我都是這樣找到一些很酷的小地方。

字彙輔助

1. go with the flow 跟著感覺走
2. take a chance 冒險、碰運氣
3. reservation 訂位、預定
4. restaurant 餐廳
5. meet 遇見、碰上、認識
6. interesting 有趣的、引起興趣的

小提點 此單元句子拓展為 6 句，可於第二次練習時，等 CD 播放到某個單字再開始跟讀，也可以隨著更熟練後，分次將跟讀時間往後至 CD 播放到第一句結束、第二句結束、第三句結束、第四句結束、第五句結束後再跟著讀，最後漸漸強化到 6 個句子唸完後再開始覆誦全部句子。

UNIT 1 ▶▶ 紐約 百老匯、美國情緣

▶▶ 聽力演練

　　由「聽力講解篇」學習了以聽數句短對話內容，然後作 shadowing 的練習，相信讀者能更熟悉 shadowing 的功用，在此章節則規劃了由聽「長句」的 shadowing 練習，由單句到一次連續聽 6 句英文並作 shadowing 的練習，學習者能從中調整自己聽英文的腳步，並在此章節紮好聽「長句」、「短段落」的基礎，更注意自己聽 CD 時的聽力專注力，為雅思聽力中 section 3 和 section 4 中學術場景的聽力作好準備，也能在實際雅思聽力時不容易走神或因題與題之間敘述過長，而在 section 4 中後段因失去耐心或誤以為自己已錯過該題「定位」而造成的失分，我們現在就一起動身，開始由聽數句「長句」開始！

※因每個讀者程度不同，若是稍具程度的讀者，可以跳過此章節喔！直接由下個篇章開始，直接作長對話的 shadowing 練習喔！

▶▶ 長句 shaowing 練習 MP3 07

※現在請跟著 CD 覆誦，練習長句 shadowing 練習，第一次先跟著 CD 以相同速度覆誦，第二次跟第三次後可以隨個人程度調整並於聽到句子內容後，拉長數秒或更長時間作練習。

KEY **1**

Coming to New York, besides exploring the city, don't miss the chance to go to one of the Broadway shows at the Broadway Theater in Manhattan. Here in New York, there are plenty of splendid Broadway shows to choose from. From the most popular show Lion King, Les Misérables, Mamma Mia, Blue Man to some of the newest shows depending on the time you go.

來到紐約除了在城市中探索，也千萬別錯過到曼哈頓百老匯劇院看一場表演的機會！在紐約，你有許多非常輝煌精彩的秀可以選擇。從很受歡迎的獅子王、悲慘世界、媽媽咪呀、藍人到許多依照你到紐約的時間而定的新秀。

字彙輔助　**1** explore 探索

　　　　　　2 splendid 輝煌精彩的

小提點　第二次練習時，可以等 CD 播放到第一個句子結束後再開始跟讀，也可以隨著更熟練後，將跟讀時間漸漸往後至 CD 播放到第二句、第三句後再開始跟讀，最後漸漸強化到一個段落唸完後再開始跟著從段落的第一句開始覆誦。

KEY 2

One thing that is almost guaranteed is that you will most likely have a memorable and unforgettable evening! There are certain think you would think that is better kept in your imagination. However, the actors in Broadway can really bring your imagination alive and even better!

有一件事是幾乎可以確定的，你非常有可能會度過一個十分印象深刻且難忘的夜晚！有些事情你會認為保有著想像空間，但是在百老匯的演員，真的可以將你的想像帶回真實世界，甚至又詮釋的更好！

字彙輔助

1 guarantee 保證

2 memorable 值得回憶的

3 unforgettable 難忘的

4 imagination 想像

小提點 第二次練習時，可以等 CD 播放到第一個句子結束後再開始跟讀，也可以隨著更熟練後，將跟讀時間漸漸往後至 CD 播放到第二句、第三句後再開始跟讀，最後漸漸強化到一個段落唸完後再開始跟著從段落的第一句開始覆誦。

KEY 3

Indeed, in the movie, "Serendipity" released in 2001, Jonathan (John Cusack) , and Sara (Kate Beckinsale) met randomly in a department store before Christmas by accident and decided to share a dessert at Serendipity III, where Sara took Jonathan because she liked the sound of "Serendipity" and also the meaning: a fortunate accident.

沒錯，在 2001 年上映的電影「美國情緣」中，強納森（約翰庫薩克飾）和莎拉（凱特貝琴薩飾）聖誕節前隨機地在一間百貨公司相遇並決定要一起去「緣III」分享一個甜點。莎拉帶強納森到那裡因為他喜歡「緣」 聽起來的聲音還有它的意思：幸運的意外。

字彙輔助　1 randomly 隨機地

　　　　　　2 fortunate 幸運的

小提點　第二次練習時，可以等 CD 播放到第一個句子結束後在開始跟讀，也可以隨著更熟練後，將跟讀時間漸漸往後至 CD 播放到第二句、第三句後再開始跟讀，最後漸漸強化到一個段落唸完後再開始跟著從段落的第一句開始覆誦。

UNIT 2 ▶▶ 倫敦 哈利波特狂熱

▶▶ 聽力演練

　　由「聽力講解篇」學習了以聽數句短對話內容，然後作 shadowing 的練習，相信讀者能更熟悉 shadowing 的功用，在此章節則規劃了由聽「長句」的 shadowing 練習，由單句到一次連續聽 6 句英文並作 shadowing 的練習，學習者能從中調整自己聽英文的腳步，並在此章節紮好聽「長句」、「短段落」的基礎，更注意自己聽 CD 時的聽力專注力，為雅思聽力中 section 3 和 section 4 中學術場景的聽力作好準備，也能在實際雅思聽力時不容易走神或因題與題之間敘述過長，而在 section 4 中後段因失去耐心或誤以為自己已錯過該題「定位」而造成的失分，我們現在就一起動身，開始由聽數句「長句」開始！

※因每個讀者程度不同，若是稍具程度的讀者，可以跳過此章節喔！直接由下個篇章開始，直接作長對話的 shadowing 練習喔！

▶▶ 長句 shadowing 練習 MP3 08

※現在請跟著 CD 覆誦，練習 5 句 shadowing 練習，第一次先跟著 CD 以相同速度覆誦，第二次跟第三次後可以隨個人程度調整並於聽到句子內容後，拉長數秒或更長時間作練習。

KEY 1

Before entering the enchanting and exciting scenes of the world-renowned Harry Potter films, loyal fans of Harry Potter will not miss the fascinating scene where Harry (Daniel Radcliffe), Ron (Rupert Grint) and Hermione (Emma Watson) have to push the trolleys through the brick wall between platform 9 and 10 to access platform 9 ¾. At 9 ¾ platform, they will be able to catch the train to go back to Hogwarts before the school year starts.

在進入世界聞名的哈利波特電影中那些神奇又刺激的畫面前,哈利波特的忠實粉絲們一定不會錯過那些有趣的場景。當哈利(丹尼爾雷得克里夫飾)、榮恩(魯博特葛林飾)和妙麗(愛瑪華森飾)必須推著推車穿過第九和第十月台中間的磚牆來到九又四分之三月台。在九又四分之三月台,他們才可以在新學年開始前搭乘火車回去霍格華滋。

字彙輔助　■ enchanting 使人著魔的
　　　　　　■ world-renowned 世界聞名的
　　　　　　■ fascinating 迷人的、極好的
　　　　　　■ trolley 推車

小提點　第二次練習時,可以等 CD 播放到第一個句子結束後開始跟讀,也可以隨著更熟練後,將跟讀時間漸漸往後至 CD 播放到第二句、第三句後再開始跟讀,最後漸漸強化到一個段落唸完後再開始跟著從段落的第一句開始覆誦。

KEY 2

The train station in all Harry Potter movies is the very Kings Cross Station in London. It has become a pretty touristy spot ever since Harry Potter movies won hearts of every household in the world.

那個在所有哈利波特電影中出現的火車站就是在倫敦的國王十字火車站。自從哈利波特贏得了世界各地人們的心之後，它就變成觀光客相當喜歡的地方。

字彙輔助 　1 touristy 觀光客喜歡的

....

小提點　第二次練習時，可以等 CD 播放到第一個句子結束後再開始跟讀，也可以隨著更熟練後，將跟讀時間漸漸往後至 CD 播放到第二句、第三句後再開始跟讀，最後漸漸強化到一個段落唸完後再開始跟著從段落的第一句開始覆誦。

KEY 3

When you arrive at Kings Cross Station, it will be pretty easy to find 9 ¾ platform and a trolley that is half way out of the wall since there is always a long line waiting for pictures taking at the site. You are allowed to take your own photo if you wish not to spend any money there.

當你到了國王十字火車站時，就會很容易就找到了九又四分之三月台，以及一個一半在牆裡的推車，因為那裡會有很長的人龍等著要拍照。如果你不想花錢的話，你也可以自己拍照。

字彙輔助　**1** platform 月台

小提點　第二次練習時，可以等 CD 播放到第一個句子結束後再開始跟讀，也可以隨著更熟練後，將跟讀時間漸漸往後至 CD 播放到第二句、第三句後再開始跟讀，最後漸漸強化到一個段落唸完後再開始跟著從段落的第一句開始覆誦。

KEY 4

You will get to pick a scarf for your photo shoot, and if you are not satisfied after that, feel free to pop in a souvenir store next door that has a Harry potter theme. Enjoy, and stay imaginative!

你可以選擇自己的哈利波特圍巾。如果拍完照後你還是不盡興的話，你也可以到隔壁以哈利波特為主題的紀念品店裡逛逛。好好玩，並且繼續保持充滿想像力！

字彙輔助　**1** pop in 作短暫的訪問、來或去一會兒
　　　　　　2 souvenir 紀念品
　　　　　　3 theme 主題
　　　　　　4 imaginative 充滿想像力的

小提點　第二次練習時，可以等 CD 播放到第一個句子結束後再開始跟讀，也可以隨著更熟練後，將跟讀時間漸漸往後至 CD 播放到第二句、第三句後再開始跟讀，最後漸漸強化到一個段落唸完後再開始跟著從段落的第一句開始覆誦。

UNIT 3 ▶▶ 洛杉磯 蜘蛛人 2

▶▶ 聽力演練

　　由「聽力講解篇」學習了以聽數句短對話內容，然後作 shadowing 的練習，相信讀者能更熟悉 shadowing 的功用，在此章節則規劃了由聽「長句」的 shadowing 練習，由單句到一次連續聽 6 句英文並作 shadowing 的練習，學習者能從中調整自己聽英文的腳步，並在此章節紮好聽「長句」、「短段落」的基礎，更注意自己聽 CD 時的聽力專注力，為雅思聽力中 section 3 和 section 4 中學術場景的聽力作好準備，也能在實際雅思聽力時不容易走神或因題與題之間敘述過長，而在 section 4 中後段因失去耐心或誤以為自己已錯過該題「定位」而造成的失分，我們現在就一起動身，開始由聽數句「長句」開始！

※因每個讀者程度不同，若是稍具程度的讀者，可以跳過此章節喔！直接由下個篇章開始，直接作長對話的 shadowing 練習喔！

▶▶ 長句 shaowing 練習 MP3 09

※現在請跟著 CD 覆誦，練習 5 句 shadowing 練習，第一次先跟著 CD 以相同速度覆誦，第二次跟第三次後可以隨個人程度調整並於聽到句子內容後，拉長數秒或更長時間作練習。

KEY 1

An amusing scene in the movie "Spider Man 2" is when Peter Parker (Toby Maguire) was running late for Mary Jane's (Kirsten Dunst) play "The Importance of Being Earnest", the usher of the theater, played by Bruce Campbell, kindly reminded Peter to tie his shoe laces, and his tie, only to find that he stopped Peter from getting in the theater to watch Mary Jane's performances for the quality of the performance.

在電影蜘蛛人 2 中其中一個好玩的一幕是當彼得帕克（陶比麥奎爾飾）去瑪麗珍（柯絲婷鄧斯特飾）所演出「真誠的重要」遲到時，由布魯斯坎貝爾飾演的劇場接待員好心提醒彼得繫他的鞋帶，以及整理他的領帶，結果在彼得照做之後，他卻因為維護表演品質而不讓彼得進入戲院看瑪麗珍的表演。

字彙輔助　**1** amusing 有趣的

小提點　第二次練習時，可以等 CD 播放到第一個句子結束後再開始跟讀，也可以隨著更熟練後，將跟讀時間漸漸往後至 CD 播放到第二句、第三句後再開始跟讀，最後漸漸強化到一個段落唸完後再開始跟著從段落的第一句開始覆誦。

KEY 2

Meanwhile, Mary Jane was performing on stage and got distracted when she saw the empty seat of Peter's in the theater. The splendid theater is the very Ivar Theatre which is located at 1605 North Ivar Avenue in Hollywood.

在同時間，瑪麗珍在台上表演時卻因為看到彼得缺席空出的空位而分心。這個華麗的戲院正是位於好萊屋區 1605 號 North Ivar 大道的 Ivar 戲院。

字彙輔助　**1** splendid 華麗的

小提點　第二次練習時，可以等 CD 播放到第一個句子結束後再開始跟讀，也可以隨著更熟練後，將跟讀時間漸漸往後至 CD 播放到第二句、第三句後再開始跟讀，最後漸漸強化到一個段落唸完後再開始跟著從段落的第一句開始覆誦。

KEY 3

The theater first opened in 1951, and several movies and plays were performed in the site. The grand theater can seat up to 350 people and during its peak, celebrities including the legendary rock star Elvis Presley performed movies in the theater.

這個戲院最早是在 1951 年開幕，這裡也有幾部戲劇和電影的演出。這個廣大的戲院可以容納 350 個人，而在它的高峰時期，許多的名人，包括傳奇的搖滾巨星貓王的電影演出也是在這裡。

字彙輔助 　1 celebrities 名人
　　　　　　2 legendary 傳奇性的

小提點 第二次練習時，可以等 CD 播放到第一個句子結束後再開始跟讀，也可以隨著更熟練後，將跟讀時間漸漸往後至 CD 播放到第二句、第三句後再開始跟讀，最後漸漸強化到一個段落唸完後再開始跟著從段落的第一句開始覆誦。

KEY 4

However, the theater had been through quite a rough ride for its survival. It later became a rock club, nudity strip club, picture-shooting rental, and it has currently been renting the theater to people for filming purposes. One regular user is the Los Angeles Film School.

然而，為了生存，這個戲院經歷了很多辛苦的歷程。它後來演變為一個搖滾夜店、脫衣舞店和拍照出租，而現在他們將戲院出租為拍片場地。一個固定的常客是洛杉磯電影學校。

字彙輔助 　1 nudity 裸露
　　　　　　2 picture-shooting 拍片
　　　　　　3 rental 租金、出租

小提點 第二次練習時，可以等 CD 播放到第一個句子結束後再開始跟讀，也可以隨著更熟練後，將跟讀時間漸漸往後至 CD 播放到第二句、第三句後再開始跟讀，最後漸漸強化到一個段落唸完後再開始跟著從段落的第一句開始覆誦。

UNIT 4 ▶▶ 聖安東尼奧 麻辣女王

▶▶ 聽力演練

　　由「聽力講解篇」學習了以聽數句短對話內容，然後作 shadowing 的練習，相信讀者能更熟悉 shadowing 的功用，在此章節則規劃了由聽「長句」的 shadowing 練習，由單句到一次連續聽 6 句英文並作 shadowing 的練習，學習者能從中調整自己聽英文的腳步，並在此章節紮好聽「長句」、「短段落」的基礎，更注意自己聽 CD 時的聽力專注力，為雅思聽力中 section 3 和 section 4 中學術場景的聽力作好準備，也能在實際雅思聽力時不容易走神或因題與題之間敘述過長，而在 section 4 中後段因失去耐心或誤以為自己已錯過該題「定位」而造成的失分，我們現在就一起動身，開始由聽數句「長句」開始！

※因每個讀者程度不同，若是稍具程度的讀者，可以跳過此章節喔！直接由下個篇章開始，直接作長對話的 shadowing 練習喔！

▶▶ 長句 shaowing 練習 MP3 10

※現在請跟著 CD 覆誦，練習 5 句 shadowing 練習，第一次先跟著 CD 以相同速度覆誦，第二次跟第三次後可以隨個人程度調整並於聽到句子內容後，拉長數秒或更長時間作練習。

聽力『講解』

聽力『演練』

聽力『實戰』

口說『演練＋實戰』

KEY 1

Miss Congeniality is a comedy released in 2000. A tomboy FBI agent Gracie Hart (Sandra Bullock) was transformed into a beauty pageant contestant to hunt down the possible suspect. It is indeed one of those ugly duckling's swan becoming movies.

麻辣女王是一部在 2000 年上映的喜劇片。一個男孩子氣的聯邦調查員葛蕾絲哈特（珊卓布拉克飾）轉變為選美比賽的參選者去捕捉一個可能的嫌犯。這的確是那些醜小鴨變天鵝的電影之一。

字彙輔助　　1 Miss Congeniality 麻辣女王

2 comedy 喜劇

3 release 上映

小提點　　第二次練習時，可以等 CD 播放到第一個句子結束後再開始跟讀，也可以隨著更熟練後，將跟讀時間漸漸往後至 CD 播放到第二句、第三句後再開始跟讀，最後漸漸強化到一個段落唸完後再開始跟著從段落的第一句開始覆誦。

KEY 2

But Hart's boyish clumsiness and kindness won hearts of many households, including the other contestants'. That's what makes her Miss Congeniality. It's the perfect film to bring you and your family a few chuckles.

但是哈特男孩子氣的笨拙和好心腸為他贏得許多人的心，包括其他參選人的。這也就是為什麼她在比賽中得到最佳人緣獎。它是一部可以帶給你和你的家人一些歡笑的片。

字彙輔助　1 clumsiness 笨拙
2 kindness 好心腸
3 congeniality 同性質、意氣相投

小提點　第二次練習時，可以等 CD 播放到第一個句子結束後再開始跟讀，也可以隨著更熟練後，將跟讀時間漸漸往後至 CD 播放到第二句、第三句後再開始跟讀，最後漸漸強化到一個段落唸完後再開始跟著從段落的第一句開始覆誦。

KEY 3

In the movie, when Hart and the other contestants are doing the swimming suit competition, it was shot at the very Arneson River Theater. It is an outdoor performance theater on the north side of the river.

在電影中，當哈特和其他參選人在競選泳裝比賽時，他們就是在艾尼遜河劇場所拍攝。這是個位在北邊河岸的戶外表演戲院。

字彙輔助 　1 contestants 參選人

....

小提點 　第二次練習時，可以等 CD 播放到第一個句子結束後再開始跟讀，也可以隨著更熟練後，將跟讀時間漸漸往後至 CD 播放到第二句、第三句後再開始跟讀，最後漸漸強化到一個段落唸完後再開始跟著從段落的第一句開始覆誦。

KEY 4

The audience usually sits on the grass-covered steps on the opposite side to enjoy the performance. There are 13 rows of seats, which can seat up to 800 audiences for a show. If you wish to see a show here, be sure to look up the performances in advance!

觀眾們通常坐在對岸，草皮覆蓋的階梯上觀賞表演。大約有十三排的座位，可以容納大概八百個觀眾。如果你想要來觀賞表演的話，記得要事先查詢有什麼表演噢！

字彙輔助 　1 audience 觀眾

....

小提點 　第二次練習時，可以等 CD 播放到第一個句子結束後再開始跟讀，也可以隨著更熟練後，將跟讀時間漸漸往後至 CD 播放到第二句、第三句後再開始跟讀，最後漸漸強化到一個段落唸完後再開始跟著從段落的第一句開始覆誦。

聽力『講解』

聽力『演練』

聽力『實戰』

口說『演練+實戰』

UNIT 5 ▶▶ 紐奧良 五星主廚快餐車

▶▶ 聽力演練

由「聽力講解篇」學習了以聽數句短對話內容，然後作 shadowing 的練習，相信讀者能更熟悉 shadowing 的功用，在此章節則規劃了由聽「長句」的 shadowing 練習，由單句到一次連續聽 6 句英文並作 shadowing 的練習，學習者能從中調整自己聽英文的腳步，並在此章節紮好聽「長句」、「短段落」的基礎，更注意自己聽 CD 時的聽力專注力，為雅思聽力中 section 3 和 section 4 中學術場景的聽力作好準備，也能在實際雅思聽力時不容易走神或因題與題之間敘述過長，而在 section 4 中後段因失去耐心或誤以為自己已錯過該題「定位」而造成的失分，我們現在就一起動身，開始由聽數句「長句」開始！

※因每個讀者程度不同，若是稍具程度的讀者，可以跳過此章節喔！直接由下個篇章開始，直接作長對話的 shadowing 練習喔！

▶▶ 長句 shaowing 練習 MP3 11

※現在請跟著 CD 覆誦，練習 5 句 shadowing 練習，第一次先跟著 CD 以相同速度覆誦，第二次跟第三次後可以隨個人程度調整並於聽到句子內容後，拉長數秒或更長時間作練習。

KEY 1

Chef is a 2004 comedy drama that captured everyone's attention with not only the joyful plot, but also the exuberance and passion of the Chef. In the film, Carl (Jon Favreau) was the head chef at a restaurant in California.

五星主廚快餐車是一部 2004 年的喜劇劇情片。它不僅以輕鬆喜悅的劇情並且以廚師的活力和熱情來抓住大家的注意力。在片中，卡爾（強費爾魯飾）是一家在加州的餐廳的主廚。

字彙輔助 **1** exuberance 豐富

小提點 第二次練習時，可以等 CD 播放到第一個句子結束後再開始跟讀，也可以隨著更熟練後，將跟讀時間漸漸往後至 CD 播放到第二句、第三句後再開始跟讀，最後漸漸強化到一個段落唸完後再開始跟著從段落的第一句開始覆誦。

KEY 2

However, he had a conflict with the restaurant owner about their never-changing "classic menu" and ended up getting a very bad review from a food critic and even quit his job as a head chef. He then started a food truck business that showed his passion for Cuban food.

然而，他和老闆對於他們從未改變的「經典菜單」起了衝突，並且因此得到一個美食評論家的負評和辭掉了主廚一職。於是他開始了他快餐車的生意，也展現了他對古巴食物的熱情。

字彙輔助　1 conflict 衝突
　　　　　　　2 classic 經典的
　　　　　　　3 review 評論

小提點　第二次練習時，可以等 CD 播放到第一個句子結束後再開始跟讀，也可以隨著更熟練後，將跟讀時間漸漸往後至 CD 播放到第二句、第三句後再開始跟讀，最後漸漸強化到一個段落唸完後再開始跟著從段落的一句開始覆誦。

KEY 3

He went on a cross-country trip with the food truck and his partner and son. The three started a bonding trip and a new chapter of their lives. In the movie, when they stopped at New Orleans, Carl took his son, Percy, to Café du Monde for their beignets.

他和他的搭擋和兒子波西踏上了一個跨越美國的快餐車旅行。三個人開始這個聯絡感情的旅程並且開始了各自人生的下一章。在電影中，當他們在紐奧良停留，卡爾帶波西到度夢咖啡館去吃法式甜甜圈（beignet)。

字彙輔助　1 New Orleans 新紐奧良
　　　　　　　2 beignet 法式甜甜圈

小提點　第二次練習時，可以等 CD 播放到第一個句子結束後再開始跟讀，也可以隨著更熟練後，將跟讀時間漸漸往後至 CD 播放到第二句、第三句後再開始跟讀，最後漸漸強化

到一個段落唸完後再開始跟著從段落的第一句開始覆誦。

KEY 4

Beignets are basically a French doughnut that is fluffy and sprinkled with sugar powder. It is not too greasy nor too sweet. Café Du Monde was opened in 1862 at the French Market. If you wish to taste the beignet as Carl and Percy did, stop by this place. Chef knows food better!

beignet 其實就是法式的甜甜圈。吃起來口感鬆軟，並且灑滿糖粉。它並不會太油膩或是過甜。度夢咖啡館是在 1862 年在法國市場開店。如果你也想要嚐嚐卡爾和波西在片中吃的法式甜甜圈，來這邊試試看。廚師比較懂美食！

字彙輔助
1 fluffy 鬆軟的
2 sprinkle 灑
3 greasy 油膩的

小提點 第二次練習時，可以等 CD 播放到第一個句子結束後再開始跟讀，也可以隨著更熟練後，將跟讀時間漸漸往後至 CD 播放到第二句、第三句後再開始跟讀，最後漸漸強化到一個段落唸完後再開始跟著從段落的第一句開始覆誦。

UNIT 6 ▶▶ 西雅圖 西雅圖夜未眠、星巴克

▶▶ 聽力演練

由「聽力講解篇」學習了以聽數句短對話內容，然後作 shadowing 的練習，相信讀者能更熟悉 shadowing 的功用，在此章節則規劃了由聽「長句」的 shadowing 練習，由單句到一次連續聽 6 句英文並作 shadowing 的練習，學習者能從中調整自己聽英文的腳步，並在此章節紮好聽「長句」、「短段落」的基礎，更注意自己聽 CD 時的聽力專注力，為雅思聽力中 section 3 和 section 4 中學術場景的聽力作好準備，也能在實際雅思聽力時不容易走神或因題與題之間敘述過長，而在 section 4 中後段因失去耐心或誤以為自己已錯過該題「定位」而造成的失分，我們現在就一起動身，開始由聽數句「長句」開始！

※因每個讀者程度不同，若是稍具程度的讀者，可以跳過此章節喔！直接由下個篇章開始，直接作長對話的 shadowing 練習喔！

▶▶ 長句 shaowing 練習 `MP3 12`

※現在請跟著 CD 覆誦，練習 5 句 shadowing 練習，第一次先跟著 CD 以相同速度覆誦，第二次跟第三次後可以隨個人程度調整並於聽到句子內容後，拉長數秒或更長時間作練習。

KEY 1

Sleepless in Seattle, a 1993 classic and still touches many people's hearts even till this day. Sam Baldwin (Tom Hanks) lost his wife to cancer and was randomly sharing the story on air in a radio show. Annie Reed (Meg Ryan) was listening to the radio show as well.

西雅圖夜未眠是一部在 1993 年上映的經典電影，但直至今日都還是觸動了很多人的心。山姆包溫（湯姆漢克飾）因為癌症失去了他的妻子，巧合之下在電台上分享了他的故事。安妮瑞德（梅格萊恩飾）正在收聽一樣的電台。

字彙輔助

1 classic 經典
2 touch 觸動
3 memory 記憶、回憶
4 randomly 隨意地

小提點　第二次練習時，可以等 CD 播放到第一個句子結束後再開始跟讀，也可以隨著更熟練後，將跟讀時間漸漸往後至 CD 播放到第二句、第三句後再開始跟讀，最後漸漸強化到一個段落唸完後再開始跟著從段落的第一句開始覆誦。

聽力『講解』

聽力『演練』

聽力『實戰』

口說『演練＋實戰』

KEY 2

The global coffee chain, Starbucks, not only serves hot and cold beverages, sandwiches, pastries, but also sells their own mugs and related products. Carrying a cup of Starbucks is more than what it looks like. It is also trendy and sometimes makes your life better. It has over 21, 000 stores in over 63 countries. Nonetheless, all big corporates must start somewhere.

這家世界連鎖咖啡店，星巴克，不只賣冷熱飲品、三明治及糕點，他們也賣自己的馬克杯和其他相關產品。拿著一杯星巴克不只是看起來這樣。這同時也是十分時髦，而且有的時候會讓你的生活更好一些。它有超過兩萬一千家店分散在六十個國家。然而，所有大企業都一定是從某個地方開始起步。

字彙輔助　**1** trendy 時髦的
　　　　　　2 corporate 企業

小提點　第二次練習時，可以等 CD 播放到第一個句子結束後在開始跟讀，也可以隨著更熟練後，將跟讀時間漸漸往後至 CD 播放到第二句、第三句後再開始跟讀，最後漸漸強化到一個段落唸完後再開始跟著從段落的一句開始覆誦。

KEY 3

This global coffee giant started its first store in 1971 at a corner of Pike Place Market. Because this is a historical district, this Starbucks gets to retain what it looked like at the beginning. One significant difference is the Starbucks logo. The one today is very different from the original one.

這個全球咖啡大咖創立於 1971 年在派克市場的轉角開了第一家店。因為這裡是歷史區，所以這家星巴克還是保有它一開始的時候的樣貌。一個很大的不同是星巴克的商標。現在的商標和最一開始的十分不同。

字彙輔助　1 global 全球的
　　　　　　2 historical 歷史的
　　　　　　3 district 地區

小提點　　第二次練習時，可以等 CD 播放到第一個句子結束後在開始跟讀，也可以隨著更熟練後，將跟讀時間漸漸往後至 CD 播放到第二句、第三句後再開始跟讀，最後漸漸強化到一個段落唸完後再開始跟著從段落的一句開始覆誦。

UNIT 1 ▶▶ 沃特金斯峽谷州立公園

▶▶ Dialogue 情境對話 🎧 MP3 13

※現在請跟著 CD 覆誦，練習一整篇完整的對話 shadowing 練習，
第一次先跟著 CD 以相同速度覆誦，第二次跟第三次後可以隨個人
程度調整並於聽到句子內容後，拉長數秒或更長時間作練習，時
間拉的越長，表示能專注聽到的對話訊息內容更多，有助於聽長
對話，例如雅思聽力 section 1 和 section 2，以及學術內容即
section 3 和 section 4 的聽力上。

Ian and Derrick are hiking at the Watkins Glen State Park, New York.	伊恩和德瑞克正在紐約的沃特金斯峽谷州立公園健行。
Ian: This place is gorgeous.	伊恩：這個地方真美。
Derrick: Yeah, this is one of the best spots around this area. I love coming out here and taking my mind off things.	德瑞克：對啊，這是這周圍最好的景點之一。我很喜歡來這裡靜一靜。

Ian: Except that you can't really do that because it's so crowded here.

伊恩：但是你不能真的靜一靜，因為這裡也太多人了吧！

Derrick: haha...no, I can't do that now. It is really crowded today.

德瑞克：哈哈……不能現在真的不行。今天真的很多人耶。

Ian: It's like an international fair or something. You can see people from everywhere here.

伊恩：這裡好像是國際園遊會還是什麼的。在這裡可以看到從到處來的人。

Derrick: Yeah, this place is a big tourist attraction.

德瑞克：對啊，這地方是一個很大的觀光景點。

Ian: It's not hard for me to see why. This place is just beautiful. We are passing under the waterfalls and going around then. How many waterfalls are there anywhere?

伊恩：這不難理解。這地方那麼漂亮。我們從瀑布下方走過，或是繞過瀑布。這裡到底有多少個瀑布啊？

Derrick: I think 19! I just looked it up the other day.

德瑞克：我想是十九個！我前幾天才查過。

Ian: And this gorge is just beautiful to look at. I wish the camera could capture its beauty, but it's just so grand for the camera to capture it all.

伊恩：而且這峽谷看起來真的很美。我真希望相機可以捕捉它的美，但是這裡真的是太大了，沒辦法全部拍不起來。

Derrick: There are a lot of professional photographers that like to come out here and take pictures. Just google them.

德瑞克：這裡有很多專業攝影師喜歡來拍照。查一查就好啦。

Ian: That's not what I meant, Derrick. I mean...it's just not gonna be the same as this right in front of us. You know what I mean?

伊恩：我不是那個意思啦！德瑞克。我的意思是說……相片跟現在在我們眼前的這個美景是不會一樣的啦。你知道我的意思嗎？

Derrick: I guess you're right. We just have to take mental pictures.

德瑞克：我想你是對的。我們只好在心裡記起來囉！

Ian: Yeah, I guess so! Get ready to get wet again, here comes another waterfall!

伊恩：對啊，我想也是！準備好被潑溼吧，又有另外一個瀑布了！

▶▶ 字彙慣用語補充包

單字	詞性	中譯	單字	詞性	中譯
gorgeous	*adj.*	華麗的、極好的	international	*adj.*	國際的
spot	*n.*	地點、場所	professional	*adj.*	專業的
crowded	*adj.*	擁擠的	mental	*adj.*	心理的

UNIT 2 ▶▶ 紐約 丘卡湖

▶▶ Dialogue 情境對話 🎧 MP3 14

※現在請跟著 CD 覆誦，練習一整篇完整的對話 shadowing 練習，第一次先跟著 CD 以相同速度覆誦，第二次跟第三次後可以隨個人程度調整並於聽到句子內容後，拉長數秒或更長時間作練習，時間拉的越長，表示能專注聽到的對話訊息內容更多，有助於聽長對話，例如雅思聽力 section 1 和 section 2，以及學術內容即 section 3 和 section 4 的聽力上。

Sammy and Tyler are visiting Tyler's family at Keuka Lake, NY in the summer.

珊米和泰勒今年夏天正在拜訪泰勒住紐約丘卡湖邊的家人。

Sammy: I can't believe you grew up at such a charming place. When you told me we were going to New York, all I could think of was the hustling bustling New York City.

珊米：我不敢相信你竟然是在這麼迷人的地方長大的。你跟我説我們要去紐約的時候，我只有想到忙碌的紐約市。

Tyler: Tell me about it. That's what everyone thinks of. Keuka Lake is one of the Finger Lakes here. Frankly, I think it's the best one. Hehe...We used to go fishing every day when we were little. I started fishing when I was five.

泰勒：就是説啊。大家都那麼想。丘卡湖是在這邊的指狀湖之一。老實説，我覺得是最棒的一個。嘿嘿……我們以前小的時候每天都會去釣魚。我從五歲就開始釣魚了。

Sammy: Really? That's incredible. That explains why you are so into fishing now. I see where that is coming from now.

珊米：真的假的？真是太棒了。難怪你現在那麼喜歡釣魚。我現在知道來源了。

Tyler: Yeah, not just that. There are so many things you can do here.

泰勒：對啊，不只有釣魚，在這裡你可以做很多事。

Sammy: What else can we do here?

珊米：在這裡我們還可以幹嘛？

Tyler: We can try wakeboarding if you're feeling adventurous.

泰勒：如果你想冒點險的話我們可以試試看滑水。或是

67

Or on a beautiful afternoon like this, my parents would take out the pontoon boat, and we would just cruise around the lake doing house window-shopping.

在像這樣美好的午後，我爸媽會一邊開著駁船漫游著湖邊，一邊瀏覽在湖邊上的房子。

Sammy: Haha, that sounds like fun!

珊米：哈哈，聽起來很好玩！

Tyler: Of course, if you are in the mood of some wine, there are plenty of fantastic wineries here as well. Apparently, the climate here is perfect for growing grapes.

泰勒：當然如果你想喝點小酒的話，這裡也有很多很棒的酒莊。很顯然這裡的氣候很適合種葡萄。

Sammy: Why not? We are on vacation. A little vino sounds great. Let me just take a shower and fresh up a little. We were on the flight for a long time. I stink.

珊米：有何不可。反正我們在度假。一點小酒聽起來很不錯。先讓我洗個澡梳洗一下。我們在飛機上超久的。我好臭喔。

Tyler: Just take a lake shower! Come on! I'll jump in with you!

泰勒：跳到湖裡洗個澡就好啦！來啦！我陪你跳進去！

Sammy: Wait...What?!

珊米：等一下……你説什麼？！

▶▶ 字彙慣用語補充包

單字	詞性	中譯	單字	詞性	中譯
charming	*adj.*	有魅力的	beautiful	*adj.*	美麗的
incredible	*adj.*	難以置信的	fantastic	*adj.*	棒極了
adventurous	*adj.*	冒險的	perfect	*adj.*	完美的、對……適合的

UNIT 3 ▶▶ 哥倫比亞錫帕基拉鹽礦大教堂

▶▶ Dialogue 情境對話 🎧 MP3 15

※現在請跟著 CD 覆誦，練習一整篇完整的對話 shadowing 練習，第一次先跟著 CD 以相同速度覆誦，第二次跟第三次後可以隨個人程度調整並於聽到句子內容後，拉長數秒或更長時間作練習，時間拉的越長，表示能專注聽到的對話訊息內容更多，有助於聽長對話，例如雅思聽力 section 1 和 section 2，以及學術內容即 section 3 和 section 4 的聽力上。

Bell and her local friend Annie are visiting the Zipaquirá Salt Cathedral in Colombia.	貝兒和她當地的朋友安妮正在哥倫比亞的錫帕基拉鹽礦大教堂裡參觀。
Bell: This cave is a salt mine?	貝兒：這個洞穴是鹽礦嗎？
Annie: Yep, to be exact, it's a cathedral. We will see some sculptures that are made of salt soon.	安妮：對啊，說仔細一點這是一個大教堂。我們很快就會看到一些用鹽做成的雕像。

Bell: Wow, this is so impressive! Look at this, this is all salt on the wall. I was so wrong. I thought this was just another huge cave.

貝兒：哇，真是太厲害了！你看這個，在牆上這些都是鹽耶。我真是誤會大了。我以為這只是另一個普通的洞穴。

Annie: Nope, it's a salt cathedral. It's actually really mind blowing to think that people did all this, I meant, dig out the salt, built the sculptures so that people can come and visit or pray.

安妮：不是喔，這是一個鹽礦大教堂。其實真的還蠻驚人的，因為人們建造這一切，我是說，挖出鹽，建造雕像讓大家都可以來這裡參觀或是祈禱。

Bell: Oh, it's dripping! Watch on for this part. It's pretty wet here.

貝兒：喔，在滴水！小心這個部分喔。這裡蠻濕的。

Annie: Thanks for the heads up! I have my hoodie on.

安妮：謝謝你的提醒！我有戴帽子。

Bell: This cave is gigantic. I feel like if I was not here with you, I would definitely get lost.

貝兒：這個洞穴也太大了吧。我覺得如果我不是因為跟你在一起的話，我一定會

迷路的。

Annie: Stop being a drama queen. There are so many tourists. All you have to do is just ask them for directions. You will be fine. Go explore a little if you want. There is a lot to see here.

貝兒：不要那麼誇張啦。這裡有那麼多觀光客。你只要跟他們問路就好啦！你會沒事的。如果你想要的話，去到處看看啊！這裡有很多可以參觀的。

Bell: I might go check out the altar at the back and pray a little.

貝兒：我想要去聖壇那裡看看，順便祈禱一下。

Annie: Okay. Go ahead and I'll be around here. Just call me if you get lost.

安妮：好啊，去吧，我會在這附近。如果你迷路的話可以打給我。

Bell: By the way, are there bats here?

貝兒：對了，這裡有蝙蝠嗎？

▶▶ 字彙慣用語補充包

單字	詞性	中譯	單字	詞性	中譯
visit	v.	參觀	gigantic	adj.	巨大的
sculpture	n.	雕刻	direction	n.	方向
impressive	adj.	令人印象深刻的	explore	v.	探索

UNIT 4 ▶▶ 黃石公園

▶▶ Dialogue 情境對話 🎧 MP3 16

※現在請跟著 CD 覆誦，練習一整篇完整的對話 shadowing 練習，第一次先跟著 CD 以相同速度覆誦，第二次跟第三次後可以隨個人程度調整並於聽到句子內容後，拉長數秒或更長時間作練習，時間拉的越長，表示能專注聽到的對話訊息內容更多，有助於聽長對話，例如雅思聽力 section 1 和 section 2，以及學術內容即 section 3 和 section 4 的聽力上。

Christie and Ben are going glamping at the Yellowstone National Park.	克里斯婷和班正要去黃石公園裡豪華露營。
Ben: What exactly is glamping anyways?	班：豪華露營到底是什麼阿？
Christie: Glamping is a blended word for glamorous camping. That's something I knew existed, but I had never tried before.	克里斯婷：豪華露營就是豪華的露營方式的混合字啦！我以前就知道有這個東西，可是從來沒有試過。但現在

But here we are!	我們在這啦！
Ben: Glamorous camping? Sounds very girly.	班：豪華的露營方式？聽起來好娘喔。
Christie: Okay relax Mr. Boy Scout. It's something different, and I just want to see what it is.	克里斯婷：好啦，放輕鬆一點，童子軍。我只是想要試試看不一樣的東西。
Ben: What happens to real camping or staying in a hotel?	班：幹嘛不真正的露營還是住在飯店就好了？
Christie: It's actually their high season right now, so they were all booked out. This was our only option, and frankly, I'm really excited to see what they have to offer.	克里斯婷：因為現在是旺季，房間都被訂光了。這是唯一還可以訂的，而且老實說，我真的還蠻期待看看他們有什麼好玩的。
Ben: Oh I see, thanks for arranging everything Christie. Yeah, this is going to be the first paid	班：喔，我了解了。謝謝你安排這些，克里斯婷。嗯，這會是我第一個要付錢的露

camping trip for me! That would be something new.

營經驗！會是全新的體驗。

Christie: Quit being so negative. We're about to have a tent with a king-size bed, a dresser, and wood-burning stove. It's going to be fun!

克里斯婷：不要那麼負面嘛。我們會有一個特大號的床，一個衣櫃，還有一個木頭火爐。一定會很好玩的！

Ben: Oh wow, how much is it a night?

班：喔哇，一個晚上要多少錢啊？

Christie: 150 dollars. Hold on, Ben, before you say anything, can I just say that all the reviews about glamping at this place are all great.

克里斯婷：一百五十元美金。等一下，班，在你説話之前，我只想説所有對這裡豪華露營的評價都很高分。

Ben: I wasn't going to say anything bad! I'm getting excited about this. Camping without doing all the work. Bravo to that!

班：我又沒有要説什麼不好的！我越來越期待了。不用做任何苦工的露營！太棒啦！

▶▶ 字彙慣用語補充包

單字	詞性	中譯	單字	詞性	中譯
glamping	*n.*	豪華露營	exist	*v.*	存在
blended	*adj.*	混和的	arrange	*v.*	安排
glamorous	*adj.*	富魅力的	negative	*adj.*	負面的

UNIT 5 ▶▶ 可愛島的懷梅阿峽谷

▶▶ Dialogue 情境對話 🎧 MP3 17

※現在請跟著 CD 覆誦，練習一整篇完整的對話 shadowing 練習，第一次先跟著 CD 以相同速度覆誦，第二次跟第三次後可以隨個人程度調整並於聽到句子內容後，拉長數秒或更長時間作練習，時間拉的越長，表示能專注聽到的對話訊息內容更多，有助於聽長對話，例如雅思聽力 section 1 和 section 2，以及學術內容即 section 3 和 section 4 的聽力上。

Eddie and Betty are at the Waimea Canyon in Kauai.	艾迪和貝蒂正在可愛島的懷梅阿峽谷。
Betty: This is the most colorful canyon I've ever seen! So red, and green, and yellow...	貝蒂：這真是我看過最富色彩的峽谷！那麼多紅色、綠色還有黃色……
Eddie: Yeah, it's beautiful. Isn't this where the movie "The Descendants" was shot? You know the one starred George Cloo-	艾迪：對啊，真的好漂亮喔。這不是「繼承人生」拍片的地方嗎？你知道就是喬治克隆尼主演的那部片子？

ney?

Betty: Oh that's right. No wonder this place looks a little familiar! I knew I have seen this from somewhere. For a moment I thought I was having a Déjà vu! That's what it is!

貝蒂：喔對喔！難怪我覺得這個地方有點眼熟。我就知道我有在哪裡看過這個地方。我就覺得似曾相似！就是那部片啦！

Eddie: Yeah, it took me a while, too. Can you imagine actors get to travel to beautiful places like this to work, and then they get millions of dollars?

艾迪：對啊，我也想了一下。你可以想像那些演員可以到這麼美的地方工作，然後他們就賺了幾百萬？

Betty: Sounds like a sweet deal to me! Too bad we're no Julia Roberts or Angelina Jolie!

貝蒂：聽起來好棒喔！真可惜我們不是茱莉亞羅柏茲還是安潔麗娜裘莉！

Eddie: I know, right. Hey! Look at those goats in the canyon! How did they get there?

艾迪：沒錯。嘿！你看那些在峽谷裡的山羊！牠們怎麼到那裡的？

Betty: Oh wow, they must have very good balance, considering they have to walk on those little heels.

貝蒂：喔哇！牠們的平衡感一定很好，而且牠們得用小小的腳後跟走路。

Eddie: Hahaha...yeah, there are a few trails around the canyon, should we give them a try?

艾迪：哈哈哈⋯⋯對啊，這裡有一些步道耶，我們要不要去試試看？

Betty: Yeah sure, I'm up to whatever!

貝蒂：好啊，我什麼都可以！

Eddie: The red dirt here is just amazing! It's so red!

艾迪：那些紅土真的很驚人耶！好紅喔！

Betty: It definitely adds the characters to this place!

貝蒂：真的為這個地方多添了一點特色。

Eddie: I'm gonna scoop some dirt home for souvenirs...

艾迪：我要挖一些土回家當紀念品⋯

▶▶ 字彙慣用語補充包

單字	詞性	中譯	單字	詞性	中譯
colorful	*adj.*	富有色彩的	imagine	*v.*	想像
star	*v.*	演出	goat	*n.*	山羊
familiar	*adj.*	熟悉的	balance	*v.*	平衡

UNIT 6 ▶▶ 阿里山日出

▶▶ Dialogue 情境對話 🎧 MP3 18

※現在請跟著 CD 覆誦，練習一整篇完整的對話 shadowing 練習，第一次先跟著 CD 以相同速度覆誦，第二次跟第三次後可以隨個人程度調整並於聽到句子內容後，拉長數秒或更長時間作練習，時間拉的越長，表示能專注聽到的對話訊息內容更多，有助於聽長對話，例如雅思聽力 section 1 和 section 2，以及學術內容即 section 3 和 section 4 的聽力上。

James and Vivian are about to watch the sunrise at Ali Mountain.	詹姆士和薇薇安正要去阿里山看日出。
James: Vivian, wake up! I made you a cup of coffee! Time to wake up and get ready to go!	詹姆士：薇薇安！起床了！我幫你泡了一杯咖啡！該起來了，我們該走了！
Vivian: I didn't sleep too well. I couldn't fall asleep all night.	薇薇安：我昨天沒睡好。我昨天晚上都睡不著。

James: Aw, we'll take a nap when we come back! Now it's time to go! We came here for the sunrise!

詹姆士：喔，我們回來的時候可以睡個午覺！現在該走了！我們來這就是要看日出的啊！

Vivian: What time is sunrise? Maybe I can sleep for another half an hour?

薇薇安：日出是幾點啊？搞不好我還可以再睡個半小時？

James: We went through all this yesterday. We have to leave here in 15 minutes!

詹姆士：我們昨天就想好了。我們必須在十五分鐘後就要出發！

Vivian: Perfect, I'll sleep for 5 more minutes. I don't need anything, so I can get ready really quickly.

薇薇安：太好了，那我再睡五分鐘。我不用準備什麼，所以我很快就可以出發了。

James: Okay, but we don't want to miss the train, and if you still want breakfast...

詹姆士：好啦，但是我們不能錯過火車，而且如果你還想要吃早餐的話……

Vivian: Alright, I'm awake. This

薇薇安：好啦，我醒了啦。

sunrise is better be good.	這個日出最好很好看。
(When they are at the top of the mountain)	（當他們登頂的時候）
Vivian: Look at the cloud. It's like ocean up here with all the colorful waves.	薇薇安：你看那個雲！在這裡好像有彩色海浪的海喔。
James: You're exactly right. They call it sea of cloud here. It's really breathtaking. Aren't you glad you woke up?	詹姆士：你講得很對。他們這裡就叫它雲海。真的很美吧。你現在有沒有很高興你有醒來？
Vivian: Sorry, I was being a drag. I was still sleeping I think.	薇薇安：對不起我早上一直拖。我那時候應該還在睡覺。
James: No problem. We made it. That's the important part!	詹姆士：沒關係啦。我們到啦。那是最重要的！

Vivian: Now what? Should we explore a little around here since we're here?

薇薇安：那現在我們要幹嘛？既然都來了，我們要不要就去到處探索一下？

James: It's my turn to get a little tired...

詹姆士：換我有點累了……

▶▶ 字彙慣用語補充包

單字	詞性	中譯	單字	詞性	中譯
sunrise	*n.*	日出	ocean	*n.*	海洋
sleep	*v.*	睡	breathtaking	*adj.*	令人屏息的
asleep	*adj.*	睡著的	important	*adj.*	重要的

UNIT 7 ▶▶ 夏威夷拉納伊島上的呼洛柏灣上露營

▶▶ Dialogue 情境對話 🎧 MP3 19

※現在請跟著 CD 覆誦，練習一整篇完整的對話 shadowing 練習，第一次先跟著 CD 以相同速度覆誦，第二次跟第三次後可以隨個人程度調整並於聽到句子內容後，拉長數秒或更長時間作練習，時間拉的越長，表示能專注聽到的對話訊息內容更多，有助於聽長對話，例如雅思聽力 section 1 和 section 2，以及學術內容即 section 3 和 section 4 的聽力上。

Tammy and Matt are camping on their honeymoon at Hulopo Bay, Lanai Island of Hawaii.	譚咪和麥特正在夏威夷的拉納伊島上的呼洛柏灣上露營度過他們的蜜月。
Tammy: I don't think I have ever been to such a private beach.	譚咪：我覺得我從來沒有來過這麼隱密的海邊。
Matt: I know what you mean. I would come here all the time, if I were someone famous.	麥特：我懂你的意思。如果我很有名的話我一定會常來這。

聽力『講解』

聽力『演練』

聽力『實戰』

口說『演練＋實戰』

Tammy: It's so perfect to camp out here. Who needs to spend a thousand dollars staying in the Four Seasons hotel?

譚咪：在這露營真是太完美了。誰需要花幾千美元去待在四季飯店？

Matt: I know, right? They have grills, picnic tables, shower, and you can actually go to the bar at the hotel. I'm sure the five star hotel is nice, but this is my kind of five star accommodation! There are only a few million more stars out here.

麥特：就是說嘛！這裡有烤肉架、野餐桌、沖澡，而且你還可以去飯店內的酒吧。我知道五星級飯店一定很棒，但這是我喜歡的那種五星級住宿！只是外面這有多幾百萬顆星星。

Tammy: That's why I married you.

譚咪：這就是為什麼我會嫁給你。

Matt: Let's set up the tent, and then we can go to the grill to fix up our dinner!

麥特：我們來搭帳篷然後去烤肉區準備我們的晚餐吧！

Tammy: I brought steak and asparagus in the cooler!

譚咪：我在小冰箱裡有帶牛排和蘆筍。

Matt: You rock Tammy! I got the blue tooth speaker, so we'll have music, too!

麥特：譚咪你最棒了！我有帶藍牙喇叭，所以我們也有音樂！

Tammy: Hey what's that dolphin sign by the beach?

譚咪：嘿，海邊旁邊的那個海豚的標示牌是什麼？

Matt: Oh, the dolphins come in this bay in the morning, but you're not supposed to swim towards the dolphins because you will disturb them. It is the dolphins' resting ground, too.

麥特：喔，早上的時候海豚會來這個灣，但是你不能朝牠們游去，因為這樣會打擾到牠們。這裡也是海豚休息的地方。

Tammy: Wow, I wish we could swim with the dolphins. That would be so amazing...Oh well...You can't have it all.

譚咪：哇，真希望我們可以跟海豚游泳。那會超棒的……哎，不可能什麼事都稱你的心。

Matt: You know...if we are out there before the dolphins come... Technically, they swim towards us...

麥特：你知道……如果我們在海豚游進來之前就在海裡……說起來的話是牠們游向我們……

▶▶ 字彙慣用語補充包

單字	詞性	中譯	單字	詞性	中譯
honeymoon	*n.*	蜜月	perfect	*adj.*	完美的
private	*adj.*	私人的	accommodation	*n.*	住宿
famous	*adj.*	著名的	disturb	*v.*	干擾

UNIT 8 ▶▶ 非洲吉力馬扎羅山健行

▶▶ Dialogue 情境對話 🎧 MP3 20

※現在請跟著 CD 覆誦，練習一整篇完整的對話 shadowing 練習，第一次先跟著 CD 以相同速度覆誦，第二次跟第三次後可以隨個人程度調整並於聽到句子內容後，拉長數秒或更長時間作練習，時間拉的越長，表示能專注聽到的對話訊息內容更多，有助於聽長對話，例如雅思聽力 section 1 和 section 2，以及學術內容即 section 3 和 section 4 的聽力上。

June went to Africa to hike Mt. Kilimanjaro and she met a girl Sofia from Denmark on the trail.	瓊去了非洲吉力馬扎羅健行，在步道上她認識了從丹麥來的蘇菲雅。
June: Are you hiking alone on this trail, too?	瓊：你也是自己來爬這個步道嗎？
Sofia: Yeah, I've always wanted to hike this trail, but no one wants to come with me, so...	蘇菲雅：對啊，我一直都很想來爬這個步道，但都沒有人要陪我來，所以……

June: That's cool. Same here! No one thought I'd really go, so I want to prove them wrong.

瓊：酷喔！我也是！沒有人覺得我真的會來，所以我想要證明他們是錯的！

Sofia: There you go, girl! We can do this. It's going to be a great experience. I'm so excited.

蘇菲雅：你辦到了我們可以的！這會是一個很棒的經驗。我好興奮喔！

June: Yeah, the only thing that worries me a little is the high altitude we're hiking into. I don't want to get the altitude sickness. That'll suck.

瓊：對啊，我唯一有點擔心的是我們會爬到高緯度的地方。我不想要得高山症！那樣就完蛋了！

Sofia: Well...at least we have a tour guide and the porters. Worst case they'll carry you down. You're so light. I'm sure they can do it!

蘇菲雅：嗯……至少我們有導遊還有挑夫。最慘的話他們也可以背你下去。你那麼輕，他們沒問題的！

June: That's comforting. Did you see how they carry the bags on their heads? They are so skilled!

瓊：我覺得安心多了。你有看到他們把包裹背在頭上的樣子嘛？超厲害的！

Sofia: I know. They must have done this trail thousands of times though.

蘇菲雅：對啊！他們一定已經爬過這個步道上千次了！

June: Yeah, I think we'll hike around 7 hours today.

瓊：對啊。我想我們今天會爬大概七個小時。

Sofia: Yep, I asked the tour guide before we came and he told me today we'll hike for around 7 hours. They brought a chef, too, so we'll eat good tonight!

蘇菲雅：對啊！我出發前有問導遊，他說今天我們大概會走七個小時。他們也有帶廚師，所以我們今天晚上應該會吃得不錯。

Sofia: I guess the only thing that surprises me is the amount of hikers here. It's so crowded. I was expecting some solo and exclusive hiking experience.

蘇菲雅：我想唯一讓我意外的是來這健行的人超多的！好多人喔！我本來想說這會是一個單獨的獨家健行體驗。

June: Haha...at least that's what the ads said, right?

瓊：哈哈⋯⋯至少他們廣告是這麼說的啦，對不對？

▶▶ 字彙慣用語補充包

單字	詞性	中譯	單字	詞性	中譯
Denmark	*n.*	丹麥	altitude	*n.*	高度
experience	*v.*	經驗	comforting	*adj.*	令人感到舒適的
excited	*adj.*	興奮的	exclusive	*adj.*	獨家的

聽力『講解』

聽力『演練』

聽力『實戰』

口說『演練+實戰』

UNIT 9 ▶▶▶ 日本深海釣魚

▶▶ Dialogue 情境對話 🎧 MP3 21

※現在請跟著 CD 覆誦，練習一整篇完整的對話 shadowing 練習，第一次先跟著 CD 以相同速度覆誦，第二次跟第三次後可以隨個人程度調整並於聽到句子內容後，拉長數秒或更長時間作練習，時間拉的越長，表示能專注聽到的對話訊息內容更多，有助於聽長對話，例如雅思聽力 section 1 和 section 2，以及學術內容即 section 3 和 section 4 的聽力上。

Pete went on a charter boat in Japan for deep sea fishing. He is talking to the fishing guide Yusuke.	彼特去日本包船出海深海釣魚。他正在和釣魚的導遊裕介聊天。
Pete: Do you guys usually catch a lot of big fish here?	彼特：你們在這通常都會釣到很多大魚嗎？
Yusuke: Yeah, there are a lot of yellowfins they get pretty big here. You'll never know. It just	裕介：對啊，這裡有很多黃鰭鮪魚，而且他們會長到蠻大的。這說不準的。今天可

might be your lucky day today!

能就是你釣到喔！

Pete: I am more than ready! Everyone has such professional setups. Hopefully, I will catch something among them.

彼得：我準備好了！大家都有好專業的設備喔。希望我可以在他們之中釣到一些什麼。

Yusuke: Fishing is not about setups. You got this Pete! I have faiths in you!

裕介：釣魚跟裝備沒什麼關係。你可以的彼特！我對你有信心！

Pete: Thanks man, I appreciate it. Oh wait, I think something is biting my bait.

彼特：謝啦！謝謝你對我的信心！等一下，好像有什麼東西在咬我的餌。

Yusuke: Really? Get ready to set the hook! Yank the pole hard the next time it bites.

裕介：真的嗎？準備好鉤住那條魚！下一次牠咬的時候用力拉魚竿。

Pete: I GOT IT!!!!

彼特：我抓到了！！！

Yusuke: Now, reel in the fish slowly, nice job Pete!

裕介：好，現在慢慢把魚拉進來，做得好彼特！

Pete: It's a fighter whatever it is. It won't let me take any line.

彼特：不管牠是什麼牠都很強壯。牠不讓我拉進任何線。

Yusuke: Keep the line tight! We want to meet the fish.

裕介：把線拉緊！我們想要看到這條魚！

(15 minutes later)

（十五分鐘後）

Yusuke: It's a Mahi! Nice work!

裕介：是一條鬼頭刀！做得好！

Pete: Oh cool!! It must be around 40 pounds!!! I'm so exhausted! I totally didn't expect catching something like this!

彼特：喔好酷喔！他應該有 40 磅（18 公斤）喔！我好累喔，我完全沒想到會釣到這個！

Yusuke: Nice catch! Put it in the

裕介：很不錯的魚耶！把牠

聽力『講解』

聽力『演練』

聽力『實戰』

口說『演練+實戰』

cooler! Now we're fishing! We still have one full day! Let's catch some more fish Pete! That was exciting watching you fight the fish!

放到冰箱裡！我們開始釣到魚囉！而且我們還有一整天！繼續釣多一點魚吧彼特！剛才看你拉這條魚進來真刺激！

Pete: The fish are totally biting here. I'm coming back every year.

彼特：在這裡魚有在咬喔！我每年都要回來釣魚！

▶▶ 字彙慣用語補充包

單字	詞性	中譯	單字	詞性	中譯
yellow	*adj.*	黃色的	faith	*n.*	信念
professional	*adj.*	專業的	reel	*v.*	拉起
setup	*n.*	設備	exciting	*adj.*	令人感到興奮的

UNIT 10 ▶▶ 哥斯大黎加的 Yoga Farm

▶▶ Dialogue 情境對話 🎧 MP3 22

※現在請跟著 CD 覆誦，練習一整篇完整的對話 shadowing 練習，第一次先跟著 CD 以相同速度覆誦，第二次跟第三次後可以隨個人程度調整並於聽到句子內容後，拉長數秒或更長時間作練習，時間拉的越長，表示能專注聽到的對話訊息內容更多，有助於聽長對話，例如雅思聽力 section 1 和 section 2，以及學術內容即 section 3 和 section 4 的聽力上。

Brie and Libbie are volunteering at Costa Rica Yoga Farm for a month this summer.	布莉和利比今年暑假正在哥斯大黎加的 Yoga Farm 當志工。
Brie: I'm so glad I came here with you! How did you even find this place anyways? We're like in the middle of a jungle.	布莉：我超高興有跟你來的！你當初怎麼找到這個的？我們真的是在叢林裡面耶。
Libbie: Oh, you know how I am always very into yoga. I was just	利比：喔，你知道我一直以來都很喜歡瑜珈。我只是隨

kind of browsing around on the Internet and just randomly saw this volunteering opportunity. I never like to be a tourist when I'm traveling, too. I'd rather stay at the place longer and blend in with the locals. So I thought this was perfect.

便在網路上逛逛然後不小心就看到這個志工的機會。我旅行的時候從來就不喜歡當觀光客。我比較喜歡在一個地方待久一點，然後跟當地人混熟。所以我看到這個就想說太完美了！

Brie: Wow, seriously? So random! I know I wouldn't have chanced it if I were you, but I'm glad you did and thanks for inviting me to come along with you! Guided yoga classes, 3 healthy meals a day, and accommodation for a month only for $550. Are you kidding me? What a steal!

布莉：哇，真的假的？超隨機的！我知道如果我是你的話我一定不會決定要來，但是我超開心你決定要來而且還約我跟你來！瑜珈課，每天三個健康餐，加上一個月的住宿才五百五十美金。開什麼玩笑！超划算的！

Libbie: What do you think about the yoga classes here?

利比：你覺得這裡的瑜伽課怎麼樣？

Brie: I love that it is a yoga class,

布莉：我很喜歡雖然這是一

but everyone kind of jumps in and shares their knowledge about yoga here. And I love the open space here. It just makes so much sense to do yoga here...Like why wouldn't you do yoga here!?

堂瑜珈課，但是大家都會加入分享他們對瑜珈的認知。而且我也很喜歡這裡開放的空間。在這裡做瑜珈超説得通的……在這裡有什麼道理不做瑜伽？！

Libbie: Haha...Yes I think you spot on about the space here. I've been doing yoga two times a day here for half a month. That's something for me.

利比：哈哈……我覺得你對這裡的空間説的真的很對。我已經每天做瑜珈兩次半個月了。對我來説真的很厲害。

Brie: Yeah, although I feel pretty self-conscious around so many yogis here. Everyone does headstand like it's nothing, but oh well, we still have half a month to go!

布莉：對啊，不過我在這麼多做瑜伽的人面前做瑜珈我都覺得很害羞。大家在做倒立好像在走廚房一樣。但好啦，我們在這還有半個月！

Libbie: That's the spirit!

利比：這個精神就對了啦！

▶▶ 字彙慣用語補充包

單字	詞性	中譯	單字	詞性	中譯
volunteer	*v.*	自願	opportunity	*n.*	機會
randomly	*adv.*	隨意地	space	*n.*	空間
accommodation	*n.*	住宿	headstand	*n.*	倒立

UNIT 11 ▶▶ 挪威的美式足球賽

▶▶ Dialogue 情境對話 🎧 MP3 23

※現在請跟著 CD 覆誦，練習一整篇完整的對話 shadowing 練習，第一次先跟著 CD 以相同速度覆誦，第二次跟第三次後可以隨個人程度調整並於聽到句子內容後，拉長數秒或更長時間作練習，時間拉的越長，表示能專注聽到的對話訊息內容更多，有助於聽長對話，例如雅思聽力 section 1 和 section 2，以及學術內容即 section 3 和 section 4 的聽力上。

Erica is taking her friend Hilda who is visiting from Norway to a college football game.	艾瑞卡要帶她從挪威來的朋友希達去參觀一場大學的美式足球賽。
Erica: Let's leave the house soon Hilda! Are you almost ready?	艾瑞卡：希達，我們要出門囉！你快準備好了嗎？
Hilda: What? When does the football game start again? I am under the impression that the game doesn't start until this	希達：什麼？你說美式足球賽什麼時候開始？我一直以為是今天晚上才要開始！

evening!

Erica: You're right, but we have to be there at 1 pm for the tailgating!	艾瑞卡：對啊，但是我們一點就要過去停車場野餐會。
Hilda: What is tailgating?	希達：停車場野餐會是什麼？
Erica: Oh my gosh, you're going to love it. It's really fun. Everyone will drive their car there to secure a spot at the parking lot, and then they'll open their trunks and just barbeque there. There will be great foods, music and drinks!	艾瑞卡：我的天啊，你一定會很愛的。真的很好玩。大家都會把他們的車開到停車場佔個好位置，然後他們就會打開後車廂，然後就在那烤肉。有好吃的食物，音樂還有喝的！
Hilda: Oh wow, it sounds like a great time! But won't you be exhausted by the time the game starts?	希達：喔哇！聽起來好好玩喔！但是等到比賽真的開始的時候大家不會就累壞了嗎？

Erica: No way, tailgating helps warming up the game! That's when you know you're going to have a great game when you tailgate.

艾瑞卡：才不會呢，停車場野餐會是幫比賽暖場！當你們有先去停車場野餐會的時候，你就知道那天的比賽會超好玩的！

Hilda: Sounds good! What should we bring? I'm clueless. This is going to be my first tailgating experience.

希達：聽起來好棒！那我們要帶什麼？我完全沒頭緒。這是我第一個停車場野餐會。

Erica: I got you covered. I've already marinated some meat and we're going to meet my friends down there. They have the grills and everything set up. We just have to show up!

艾瑞卡：有我在，別擔心。我已經醃了一些肉，然後我們會去跟我的一些朋友會合。他們已經把烤肉架還有其他東西架好了，我們只要出現就好了！

Hilda: Excellent!

希達：太棒了！

▶▶ 字彙慣用語補充包

單字	詞性	中譯	單字	詞性	中譯
college	n.	學院、大學	exhausted	adj.	筋疲力盡的
impression	n.	印象	clueless	adj.	沒頭緒的
tailgating	n.	停車場野餐會	excellent	adj.	傑出的

▶▶ Dialogue 情境對話 🎧 MP3 24

※現在請跟著 CD 覆誦，練習一整篇完整的對話 shadowing 練習，第一次先跟著 CD 以相同速度覆誦，第二次跟第三次後可以隨個人程度調整並於聽到句子內容後，拉長數秒或更長時間作練習，時間拉的越長，表示能專注聽到的對話訊息內容更多，有助於聽長對話，例如雅思聽力 section 1 和 section 2，以及學術內容即 section 3 和 section 4 的聽力上。

Nina and Lavery are hiking to the Kealakekua Bay, Big Island, for snorkeling.	妮娜和拉佛立正要去夏威夷大島的凱阿拉凱庫灣浮潛。
Nina: This isn't a bad hike at all. I don't get why people are so intimidated about hiking down this trail.	妮娜：這個步道一點都不會不好啊。我不懂為什麼大家那麼怕來爬這個步道。
Lavery: Well, we are going downhill now, so naturally it's	拉佛立：嗯，因為我們現在在走下坡啊，所以當然很簡

easy. Wait till we have to climb back up the hills.

單。等我們爬上坡的時候你就知道了。

Nina: If you're trying to scare me, it's working. It is pretty steep, too. I can't imagine having to climb back up. How far is this trail anyways?

妮娜：如果你是想要嚇我的話，很有用喔！而且這裡蠻陡的。我無法想像要爬回來。這個步道到底多長啊？

Lavery: I'm not exactly sure, but there are 8 markers in total, and each is around ¼ mile or more.

拉佛立：我也不太確定，但是這裡總共有八個標示牌。每一個都大概四分之一英里（四百公尺）以上。

Nina: What?! And all this time, we've only passed 1 marker?

妮娜：什麼！？我們到目前為止只有經過一個標示牌？

Lavery: Yep,I'm not trying to scare you, but I just want to prepare you.

拉佛立：對啊，我沒有要嚇你啦，我只是想要讓你有心理準備。

(1 hour and half later)

（一個半小時後）

Nina: The snorkeling is better to be good here!! I'm soooo ready to jump in the water.

妮娜：這裡的浮潛最好很棒！我已經超級無敵準備好要跳到水裡了。

Lavery: Let's do it. The visibility of the water seems amazing today!

拉佛立：我們走吧！今天水裡的能見度超棒的！

Nina: Oh wait a minute, are those sharks?? Look at those fins!!

妮娜：等等，那些是鯊魚嗎？你看那些鰭！

Lavery: No, that's an eagle ray! Today is our lucky day! They look just like angels when they are swimming!

拉佛立：不是啦，那些是燕魟！我們今天真幸運！牠們在游泳的時候看起來會很像天使！

Nina: Are those dangerous?

妮娜：牠們會危險嗎？

Lavery: No, not at all. They are not aggressive! Cross my heart.

拉佛立：不會啦，一點都不會。牠們沒有攻擊性！我保證。

Nina: Okay, let me get my fins and snorkels ready.

妮娜：好，讓我穿一下我的蛙鞋和浮潛裝備。

Lavery: Dolphins!! I'm going in first Nina! I'll see you on the flipside!

拉佛立：海豚！我要先跳下去了喔妮娜！待會見！

Nina: Wait up!

妮娜：等我一下啦！

▶▶ 字彙慣用語補充包

單字	詞性	中譯	單字	詞性	中譯
snorkeling	*n.*	浮潛	imagine	*v.*	想像
intimidated	*adj.*	威脅的	dangerous	*adj.*	危險的
downhill	*n.*	下坡	aggressive	*adj.*	具侵略性的

UNIT 13 ▶▶ 舊金山的酒吧

▶▶ Dialogue 情境對話 🎧 MP3 25

※現在請跟著 CD 覆誦，練習一整篇完整的對話 shadowing 練習，第一次先跟著 CD 以相同速度覆誦，第二次跟第三次後可以隨個人程度調整並於聽到句子內容後，拉長數秒或更長時間作練習，時間拉的越長，表示能專注聽到的對話訊息內容更多，有助於聽長對話，例如雅思聽力 section 1 和 section 2，以及學術內容即 section 3 和 section 4 的聽力上。。

Jessica and Sam are going to the Open Mic night at a bar in San Francisco.	潔西卡和山姆正要去舊金山的一間酒吧參加 Open Mic（開放式麥克風）。
Jessica: Are you going to perform tonight?	潔西卡：你今天晚上要表演嗎？
Sam: I don't know. I guess we'll see what the vibe is like tonight.	山姆：我不知道耶。我想我們先看看今天晚上的氣氛怎麼樣好了。

Jessica: Oh, it's going to be great, and I'll be your biggest fan and make lots of noises.

潔西卡：喔，會很棒的啦，而且我會當你最大的粉絲，然後製造很多噪音。

Sam: Haha...thanks Jessica, but that sounds horrible.

山姆：哈哈……謝啦潔西卡，但是聽起來很恐怖。

Jessica: Come on, Sam, you're such a great musician. You and your guitar are going to go far. Someone has to discover you.

潔西卡：拜託，山姆，你是那麼厲害的樂手耶。你和你的吉他一定會有很長的路可以走的。你應該要被挖掘的。

Sam: Thanks Jessica. You know what, I'll go if you go.

山姆：謝啦潔西卡。你知道怎樣嘛，如果你上台的話，我就上台。

Jessica: What, no way, I can't Acapella it.

潔西卡：什麼，才不要。我不會清唱啦。

Sam: I'll play guitar for you. Let's just do what we normally do. That sounds really good.

山姆：我會幫你彈吉他。我們就像平常那樣表演就好啦。那樣聽起來很棒。

Jessica: We were just fooling around though. Nobody wants to see me on stage.

潔西卡：我們只是在胡鬧而已耶。沒有人想看我上台啦。

Sam: I DO! It will be fun Jessica. You can play the drum, too. Let's jam!

山姆：我想啊！一定會很好玩的潔西卡。你也可以打鼓啊！我們來演奏啦！

Jessica: Alright, that sounds fun. Just like the vocal in Echosmith, huh? She always sings and plays drums.

潔西卡：好啦，聽起來蠻好玩的。就像史密斯迴聲樂團裡面的主唱一樣。她每次都一邊唱一邊打鼓。

Sam: There you go! I'm gonna go tell the manager here that we're performing.

山姆：那就對啦！我去跟這裡的經理說一下我們要上台。

Jessica: Oh my god Sam. We're leaving San Francisco tomorrow anyways.

潔西卡：我的天啊山姆。反正我們明天就要離開舊金山了。

Sam: You only live once! Let's

山姆：人生只有一次。我們

do it.

上台吧。

Jessica: Maybe we'll have some fans that don't want us to leave.

潔西卡：搞不好我們還會有一些粉絲不想要我們離開。

Sam: hahaha...I'm ready for some fun!

山姆：哈哈哈……我已經準備好要好好玩一下了！

▶▶ 字彙慣用語補充包

單字	詞性	中譯	單字	詞性	中譯
perform	*v.*	表演	discover	*v.*	發現
vibe	*n.*	氣氛、情境	normally	*adv.*	通常地
horrible	*adj.*	可怕的	manager	*n.*	經理

UNIT 14 ▶▶ 西班牙的布尼奧爾蕃茄節

▶▶ Dialogue 情境對話 🎧 MP3 26

※現在請跟著 CD 覆誦，練習一整篇完整的對話 shadowing 練習，第一次先跟著 CD 以相同速度覆誦，第二次跟第三次後可以隨個人程度調整並於聽到句子內容後，拉長數秒或更長時間作練習，時間拉的越長，表示能專注聽到的對話訊息內容更多，有助於聽長對話，例如雅思聽力 section 1 和 section 2，以及學術內容即 section 3 和 section 4 的聽力上。

Jasmine and Ray are in Buñol, Spain for the Tomato Festival (La Tomatina in Spanish).	潔斯敏和雷在西班牙的布尼奧爾參加蕃茄節。
Jasmine: Oh my god, Ray, I cannot believe how many people there are here.	潔斯敏：我的天阿，雷，我不敢相信有這麼多人在這裡。
Ray: I know, according to the radio we listened to on the way here, there are going to be	雷：對啊！我們剛剛來的路上聽的電台有說今天會有五萬人從世界各地來參加。

about 50, 000 participants from all over the world today.

Jasmine: I'm so excited about this huge food fight! We should probably buy the goggles and gloves people are selling. That sounds like a good idea.

潔斯敏：我好期待這個超大的食物大戰喔！我們應該要買個這邊在賣的護目鏡和手套。好像是一個還不錯的點子。

Ray: Yeah, I agree with you. Look around us. There are tour buses all over the place. I recognize the Russian and Japanese languages on the buses. This is a bigger event than I imagined it.

雷：對啊，我也這麼覺得。你看看我們週遭到處都有觀光巴士耶。我有認出巴士上的俄文還有日文。這是一個比我想像還要大很多的活動耶。

Jasmine: I know, right? We should probably head over to the plaza where the festival takes place.

潔斯敏：對啊！我們應該要朝著丟蕃茄的廣場前進了。

Ray: Yeah, we should, if we can pass all these people in front of

雷：對啊，我們應該要的，如果我們可以超過我們前面

us.

這些人的話。

Jasmine: Look Ray, what's that person doing climbing up the wooden pole up there?

潔斯敏：雷你看！那個人爬上那個木頭的柱子要幹嘛？

Ray: It's the tradition. The festival starts when some brave soul reaches the ham at the top of the greased-up pole. It is very challenging in my opinion.

雷：喔那是傳統啊！如果某個很勇敢的人可以爬上這個抹了油的柱子，然後把上面的火腿拿下來的話，蕃茄節就會正式開始。我覺得超難的。

Jasmine: Well, that's a lot of pressure on him! What happens if no one can do it?

潔斯敏：喔，那對那個人來說壓力好大喔！如果沒人可以做到呢？

Ray: Well, it's only for the entertaining purpose. The festival will start whether anyone reaches the ham or not.

雷：喔其實那只是為了娛樂效果啦！蕃茄節不管有沒有人可以拿得到火腿都會開始啦！

Jasmine: Oh, what a relief. The festival will start in any second now!

潔斯敏：喔，真讓人鬆一口氣。那番茄節就隨時都會開始了耶！

Ray: Make sure you crush your tomatoes before you throw at anyone! And you know what makes it even more fun?

雷：你在丟番茄前一定要先把番茄捏碎喔！而且你知道怎麼樣會更好玩嗎？

Jasmine: What?

潔斯敏：怎麼樣？

Ray: If you just secretly aim at the same person the whole time...

雷：如果你一直偷偷瞄準同一個人丟的話……

▶▶ 字彙、慣用語補充包

單字	詞性	中譯	單字	詞性	中譯
participants	*n.*	參加者	plaza	*n.*	廣場
goggles	*n.*	護目鏡	challenging	*adj.*	挑戰的
gloves	*n.*	手套	secretly	*adv.*	秘密地

UNIT 15 ▶▶ 傑克島袋的烏克麗麗音樂會

▶▶ Dialogue 情境對話 🎧 MP3 27

※現在請跟著 CD 覆誦，練習一整篇完整的對話 shadowing 練習，第一次先跟著 CD 以相同速度覆誦，第二次跟第三次後可以隨個人程度調整並於聽到句子內容後，拉長數秒或更長時間作練習，時間拉的越長，表示能專注聽到的對話訊息內容更多，有助於聽長對話，例如雅思聽力 section 1 和 section 2，以及學術內容即 section 3 和 section 4 的聽力上。

Jake Shimabukuro was touring in Japan. Aaron and his friend Miyu are at his Ukulele concert.	傑克島袋正在日本巡迴表演。艾倫和他的朋友成美正在傑克島袋的烏克麗麗音樂會裡。
Aaron: He is one of the best ukulele players I know. I'm really excited we can come to this.	艾倫：他是我知道最厲害的烏克麗麗樂手之一。我真的很興奮我們可以來這裡。
Miyu: Me, too. Luckily we got the tickets. I know a lot of my	成美：我也是。我們真的很幸運可以買得到票耶。我知

friends were trying so hard to come, but they couldn't get any tickets.

道我有很多朋友超想要來的，可是都買不到票。

Aaron: I didn't realize he's big in Japan, too!

艾倫：我不知道原來他在日本也那麼紅！

Miyu: Yeah, he is! Hey here we go!!! He's playing!!

成美：對啊，他真的很紅！嘿開始了！他在演奏了！！

Aaron: It's so amazing how fast he's playing the ukulele. I can't even see his fingers.

艾倫： 他可以彈烏克麗麗彈得那麼快真的很厲害耶！我都看不到他的手指。

Miyu: I know, and it is so different than the regular ukulele performances. It's like that's coming out from another instrument!

成美：對啊，而且他跟一般的烏克麗麗樂手差好多喔。好像他在彈不一樣的樂器一樣。

Aaron: Yes, his strumming is so energetic and powerful. I wish I

艾倫：對啊，他的彈奏真的好有活力又很有力。我真希

could play like him.

望我可以彈得跟他一樣。

Miyu: I just wish I could even play anything.

成美：我只希望我會彈就好了。

Aaron: Well, that's not hard, is it? There are a lot of places offering lessons.

艾倫：嗯，那不難吧？現在有很多地方都可以學啊！

Miyu: You're right, maybe I should take a lesson and give it a shot.

成美：你說的對啦，或許我該去上個課試試看。

Aasron: You should, and then maybe you can take me on your tours around the world.

艾倫：你應該要去學的，說不定以後你就可以帶我到處去你的世界巡迴演出。

Miyu: Haha...thanks for the pep talk. But it's going to be a long wait. I'm not the brightest when it comes to music.

成美：哈哈……謝謝你的鼓勵啊！不過你可能要等很久。我沒有什麼音樂細胞。

Aaron: Well...you've got to start somewhere, right? | 艾倫：嗯嗯……不過還是得有個開始啊，對吧？

Miyu: True that. Now can we enjoy the show, my life coach? | 成美：你說的對啦。那我們現在可不可以開始享受這個表演啊，人生導師？

Aaron: Yes, ma'am. | 艾倫：是的，小姐。

▸▸ 字彙慣用語補充包

單字	詞性	中譯	單字	詞性	中譯
ticket	*n.*	票	**regular**	*adj.*	一般的
realize	*v.*	了解	**strum**	*v.*	彈奏
amazing	*adj.*	驚人的	**enjoy**	*v.*	享受

UNIT 16 ▶▶ 洛杉磯的迪士尼樂園

▶▶ Dialogue 情境對話 🎧 MP3 28

※現在請跟著 CD 覆誦，練習一整篇完整的對話 shadowing 練習，第一次先跟著 CD 以相同速度覆誦，第二次跟第三次後可以隨個人程度調整並於聽到句子內容後，拉長數秒或更長時間作練習，時間拉的越長，表示能專注聽到的對話訊息內容更多，有助於聽長對話，例如雅思聽力 section 1 和 section 2，以及學術內容即 section 3 和 section 4 的聽力上。

Summer and Royce are at Disneyland in Los Angeles.	夏天和羅伊斯正在洛杉磯的迪士尼樂園。
Royce: It just amazes me that there are so many people in Disneyland.	羅伊斯：迪士尼樂園有這麼多的人真是令我傻眼。
Summer: It is Disneyland that you are talking about. What do you expect? That everyone hates Mickey Mouse and Fro-	夏天：畢竟你說的是迪士尼樂園啊！不然你以為是怎麼樣？大家都討厭米老鼠還有冰雪奇緣嗎？

zen?

Royce: I get your points, but I can't help but wonder how much Disneyland is making.

羅伊斯：我知道你的意思，但我只是很好奇迪士尼到底賺了多少錢。

Summer: The tickets are so pricy, too. Dreams are not cheap nowadays.

夏天：票也超貴的。現在買一個夢真的不便宜。

Royce: No, they aren't. Well, where do you want to go? It looks like we have to wait for a long time anywhere we go anyways, so just pick one.

羅伊斯：真的不便宜。嗯，你想要去哪裡啊？看來到處都要排很久的樣子，所以隨便你選一個吧。

Summer: Follow me, Royce. Let's go find the fast pass machine and get the fast passes.

夏天：跟我走，羅伊斯。我們去找快速通行卡的機器，然後拿快速通行卡。

Royce: What are those for? I thought we already got tickets?

羅伊斯：那是要幹嘛的？我以為我們已經買好票了？

Summer: It's pretty much a ticket that puts us in line. There will be a return time, and we just have to come back at the time the ticket indicates. We can skip the whole waiting process. At least the very long waits anyways.

夏天：其實就是一個幫我們排隊的票啦。上面會註明回來的時間，然後我們就只要在票上指示的時間回來就好了。我們可以跳過整個排隊的過程。至少跳過那些等很久的啦。

Royce: That's genius. We just have to get all the fast passes and figure out where to go first.

羅伊斯：好聰明喔。所以我們就只要去拿那些快速通行卡，然後再看要先去哪一個就好了。

Summer: Yep, it's simple as that. It's amazing how much time you can actually save.

夏天：對啊，就是那麼簡單。你會很驚訝我們可以省下多少時間。

Royce: I'm surprised not more people know about this.

羅伊斯：我很驚訝沒有更多人知道這東西。

Summer: Hurray for us!

夏天：對我們來說超棒的啊！

▶▶ 字彙慣用語補充包

單字	詞性	中譯	單字	詞性	中譯
amaze	v.	驚訝	figure out		了解
expect	v.	期待	simple	adj.	簡單的
pricy	adj.	昂貴的	amazing	adj.	驚人的

UNIT 17 ▶▶ 墨西哥的迪士尼遊輪

▶▶ Dialogue 情境對話　🎧 MP3 29

※現在請跟著 CD 覆誦，練習一整篇完整的對話 shadowing 練習，第一次先跟著 CD 以相同速度覆誦，第二次跟第三次後可以隨個人程度調整並於聽到句子內容後，拉長數秒或更長時間作練習，時間拉的越長，表示能專注聽到的對話訊息內容更多，有助於聽長對話，例如雅思聽力 section 1 和 section 2，以及學術內容即 section 3 和 section 4 的聽力上。

Brent and Rochelle are on the Disney Cruise from Florida to Mexico.	布蘭特和若雪兒正在從佛羅里達出發要到墨西哥的迪士尼遊輪上。
Rochelle: Thank you so much for agreeing to come to this with me!	若雪兒：謝謝你願意跟我一起來！
Brent: This is actually really fun. The AquaDuck Water Coaster is so fun!! At one point the slide	布蘭特：這裡其實還蠻好玩的。那個超級滑水梯超好玩的！而且它中間有某一段甚

even goes out of the ship! I'm really impressed.

至還超出了船身！我覺得蠻厲害的。

Rochelle: See, I told you it won't be that bad!

若雪兒：看吧！我就跟你説沒那麼糟了！

Brent: Hey don't push it! I said it's fun already. You do notice that we are the only adults without kids here.

布蘭特：嘿嘿不要得寸進尺喔！我就説很厲害了。你有注意到我們是唯一沒有帶小孩來的大人。

Rochelle: We think young! Should we go try how to edit and produce a film? Who knows, maybe we can make the next best Disney movie!

若雪兒：我們是思想年輕！我們要不要去試試看編輯製作一部片？誰知道，我們可能會作出迪士尼下一部大作耶！

Brent: Yep, we like to think positively, too! I hate to admit it, but I kind of enjoy this.

布蘭特：對啊，我們思想也很樂觀。我是很不想承認，可是我還蠻喜歡這的。

Rochelle: Just to be fair, we can

若雪兒：公平起見，我們等

go grab a drink at the bar later.

下可以去酒吧喝一杯。

Brent: Oh wow, who is the grown-up here? I almost forgot she came to this cruise with me, too!

布蘭特：喔哇！這個大人是誰？我都忘了她也有跟我來這個遊輪。

Rochelle: I should probably change my mind.

若雪兒：還是我應該要改變主意。

Brent: No, you shouldn't. That was a brilliant idea! Good job Rochelle! I'm proud of you! Now let's make some film and go grab a drink afterwards.

布蘭特：不用，你不應該要改變主意。那是一個超棒的主意。做得好若雪兒！我以你為榮！現在我們去製片，然後去喝一杯吧！

Rochelle: You're the best!

若雪兒：你最好了！

Brent: I don't know what you're talking about!

布蘭特：我不知道你在說什麼！

▶▶ 字彙慣用語補充包

單字	詞性	中譯	單字	詞性	中譯
cruise	*n.*	巡航；航遊	grab	*v.*	抓住
impress	*v.*	留下印象	change	*v.*	改變
adult	*n.*	成人	brilliant	*adj.*	光輝的、明亮的

UNIT 18 ▶▶ 京都藝妓藝廊

▶▶ Dialogue 情境對話 🎧 MP3 30

※現在請跟著 CD 覆誦，練習一整篇完整的對話 shadowing 練習，第一次先跟著 CD 以相同速度覆誦，第二次跟第三次後可以隨個人程度調整並於聽到句子內容後，拉長數秒或更長時間作練習，時間拉的越長，表示能專注聽到的對話訊息內容更多，有助於聽長對話，例如雅思聽力 section 1 和 section 2，以及學術內容即 section 3 和 section 4 的聽力上。

Jean and her friend Barbara are at a Geisha makeover studio in Kyoto.	珍和她的朋友芭芭拉在京都一間藝妓藝廊裡改裝變身中。
Jean: Wow, I'm so excited that we get to do this!	珍：哇，我好興奮我們可以來做這個行程喔！
Barbara: I know, this would be something different and definitely unique to do while we are here. You asked me about tradi-	芭芭拉：對啊！這會是不一樣的經驗，而且也一定會是我們在這裡很獨特的經驗。你前幾天不是在問我關於傳

tional costumes here the other day, so I had this idea!

統服飾的問題，我是從那裡得到靈感要做這個的！

Jean: I love it. So wait, how long does the makeover take? I'm just trying to think if it's worth the money.

珍：我超愛的。啊等一下，所以這個改裝要多久啊？我只是要想想看這樣划不划算。

Barbara: It'll take about 2 hours they said. And then we have the photo-shoots with the local professional photographer here.

芭芭拉：他們說會花大約兩個小時的時間，然後當地的一些專業攝影師會幫我們拍一些照片。

Jean: 2 hours just for putting on the make up and dress? That's crazy!

珍：兩個小時只是在化妝跟穿衣服？好誇張！

Barbara: Yeah, I don't think the photo shoots will take long at all though.

芭芭拉：對啊，不過我不覺得拍照會花很久的時間。

Jean: I hope not, but oh well,

珍：我希望不會，但是，我

聽力『講解』
聽力『演練』
聽力『實戰』
口說『演練＋實戰』

then we'll get a sense of how it is to be a real Geisha.

們會知道真正當一個藝妓是什麼感覺。

Barbara: Can you imagine the amount of makeup they are going to put on our face though? We're gonna be completely white!

芭芭拉：你可以想像他們要在我們臉上化多少妝嗎？我們會變超白的。

Jean: Oh this is going to be great! I'm definitely going to take some funny photos.

珍：喔，這一定會很好玩！我一定要拍一些好笑的照片。

Barbara: Let's do a talent show, too. I'll videotape it. It'll be so fun!

芭芭拉：我們來做才藝表演啦！我來錄影！一定會很好玩！

Jean: A talent show. Hold on a minute. This is getting complicated.

珍：才藝表演。等一下，事情怎麼變得越來越複雜了。

▶▶ 字彙慣用語補充包

單字	詞性	中譯	單字	詞性	中譯
Geisha	*n.*	藝妓	costumes	*n.*	服飾
unique	*adj.*	獨特的	videotape	*v.*	錄影
traditional	*adj.*	傳統的	complicated	*adj.*	複雜的

UNIT 19 ▶▶ 夏威夷巴西莓果冰沙

▶▶ Dialogue 情境對話 🎧 MP3 31

※現在請跟著 CD 覆誦，練習一整篇完整的對話 shadowing 練習，第一次先跟著 CD 以相同速度覆誦，第二次跟第三次後可以隨個人程度調整並於聽到句子內容後，拉長數秒或更長時間作練習，時間拉的越長，表示能專注聽到的對話訊息內容更多，有助於聽長對話，例如雅思聽力 section 1 和 section 2，以及學術內容即 section 3 和 section 4 的聽力上。

Mia and her local friend Leilani are going to the local health bar for Acai Bowl in Hawaii.	蜜雅和她當地的好朋友蕾拉妮要去夏威夷一間健康飲食店買 Acai Bowl（巴西莓果冰沙）。
Leilani: I'm gonna take you to try one of the things I love in the world.	蕾拉妮：我要帶你去品嚐一個我全世界最喜歡吃的東西之一。
Mia: I'm excited. What is it? We're going surfing later. I don't	蜜雅：我好期待喔！我們要吃什麼啊？我們等下要去衝

want to be too stuffed.

浪耶。我不想要吃太飽。

Leilani: It's called "Acai Bowl". It's a smoothie made from Acai berries, which has a lot of natural antioxidants, and on top of the smoothie, they put fresh blueberries, strawberries, bananas, granola and honey. It's actually pretty filling, but doesn't make you feel too stuffed.

蕾拉妮：我們要吃的東西叫做「巴西莓果冰沙」。它是一種用有很多天然抗氧化劑的巴西莓果做成的冰沙，然後在冰沙上面，他們會放新鮮的藍莓、草莓、香蕉、穀片，還有蜂蜜。吃完其實會飽，可是不會讓你太脹。

Mia: Wow, that sounds amazing and so healthy at the same time!

蜜雅：哇！聽起來好棒喔，而且又很健康！

Leilani: Yeah, it's very healthy and it's actually pretty perfect to eat this before surfing. It gives you energy, and it's relatively light.

蕾拉妮：對啊！超健康的，而且其實蠻適合在衝浪之前吃的！它會給你能量，而且相比之下熱量又不會太高。

Mia: Let's give it a try. | 蜜雅：我們快來試試看吧。

(After they get their Acai Bowl) | （在他們拿到巴西莓果冰沙之後）

Leilani: So what do you think? | 蕾拉妮：你覺得怎麼樣？

Mia: It's even better than what I expected. They are not stingy giving out all these fresh fruits! | 蜜雅：比我想像的還要好吃！他們給新鮮水果一點也不小氣！

Leilani: No way, that's one of the selling points! | 蕾拉妮：當然不會啊，那是他們的賣點之一！

Mia: I wish we had this back home, too! Can you make this at home? | 蜜雅：我真希望我們家那裡也有賣這個！你可以在家自己做這個嗎？

Leilani: Yeah, usually we can find the frozen Acai berries at local supermarkets, so we just | 蕾拉妮：可以啊！通常可以在當地的超市買到冷凍的巴西莓果，所以有時候就可以

make them at home sometimes. But of course it's easier to buy one, if you don't crave it every day.

在家自製冰沙。但是如果你不是天天想吃的話，當然直接去買會比較簡單。

Mia: I have to look this up. It's perfect to substitute for some unhealthy meals I have.

蜜雅：我要來查一下。我覺得如果用這個來取代我一些不健康的飲食的話會很好！

Leilani: Goodbye McDonald's!

蕾拉妮：拜拜麥當勞！

▶▶ 字彙慣用語補充包

單字	詞性	中譯	單字	詞性	中譯
local	*adj.*	當地的	amazing	*adj.*	驚人的
natural	*adj.*	自然的	substitute	*n.*	替代物
antioxidant	*n.*	抗氧化物	unhealthy	*adj.*	不健康的

UNIT 20 ▶▶ 納帕品酒

▶▶ Dialogue 情境對話 🎧 MP3 32

※現在請跟著 CD 覆誦，練習一整篇完整的對話 shadowing 練習，第一次先跟著 CD 以相同速度覆誦，第二次跟第三次後可以隨個人程度調整並於聽到句子內容後，拉長數秒或更長時間作練習，時間拉的越長，表示能專注聽到的對話訊息內容更多，有助於聽長對話，例如雅思聽力 section 1 和 section 2，以及學術內容即 section 3 和 section 4 的聽力上。

Caroline and Brandon are doing wine tasting at Napa Valley.	凱若林和布蘭登正在納帕品酒。
Caroline: Yay, we made it! Aren't you glad that we made a reservation now? This place is packed!	凱若林：耶！我們終於到了！你現在有沒有很高興我們有先預約？這裡超多人的！
Brandon: Yes, I am indeed. Thanks again for planning this for us Caroline.	布蘭登：有啦！我真的很高興我們有先預約。再次謝謝你幫我們安排這個行程啊凱

若林。

Caroline: No problem. I also did a little bit research on their wine here. There are a lot of wines to try in this winery, so I think our game plan should be picking different wines and then we can try many different ones.

凱若林：沒什麼啦！我也有查了一下這裡的酒。這個酒莊有超多酒可以試的，所以我覺得我們的戰術應該是要挑不一樣的酒試喝，然後我們就可以喝到很多不一樣的了。

Brandon: Yes, your honor. No objections to that!

布蘭登：好的庭上。我沒有異議。

(They started wine tasting)

（他們開始品酒）

Caroline: How do you like yours?

凱若林：你喜歡你的嗎？

Brandon: I like the nutty finish on this Sauvignon Blanc. It's really perfect for a hot day like this. How's yours?

布蘭登：我喜歡這款最後有堅果香味的白蘇維濃酒。在像今天那麼熱的天氣，喝這種酒真是太棒了。

Caroline: My Cabernet Sauvignon is really smooth. I can totally see this one pair well with steak. Yum! Should we get a bottle of this? We'll enjoy it.

凱若林：我的卡本內蘇維濃喝起來真的很順。我覺得拿這個搭牛排一定很配。好吃耶！我們要不要買一瓶？我們一定會很喜歡。

Brandon: Is that your favorite out of all though? I kind of like the Chardonnay at the beginning the best.

布蘭登：可是那是你裡面最喜歡的一瓶嗎？我好像最喜歡一開始的那瓶夏多內。

Caroline: I like that one, too, but it's a bit too dry for me I think.

凱若林：我也喜歡那瓶，可是我覺得對我來說味道有點太淡了。

Brandon: Alright then, let's get a bottle of the Cabernet Sauvignon. Let's bag a little San Francisco home.

布蘭登：好吧！那我們就買一瓶卡本內蘇維濃吧！打包一點舊金山回家！

▶▶ 字彙慣用語補充包

單字	詞性	中譯	單字	詞性	中譯
reservation	n.	訂位	different	adj.	不同的
plan	n.	計畫	objection	n.	反對
pick	v.	選擇	smooth	adj.	平順的

UNIT 21 ▶▶ 雪梨的維多利亞購物中心

▶▶ Dialogue 情境對話 🎧 MP3 33

※現在請跟著 CD 覆誦，練習一整篇完整的對話 shadowing 練習，
第一次先跟著 CD 以相同速度覆誦，第二次跟第三次後可以隨個人
程度調整並於聽到句子內容後，拉長數秒或更長時間作練習，時
間拉的越長，表示能專注聽到的對話訊息內容更多，有助於聽長
對話，例如雅思聽力 section 1 和 section 2，以及學術內容即
section 3 和 section 4 的聽力上。

Cecilia and Gracie are shopping around at Queen Victoria Building in Sydney.	西西利雅和葛雷絲正在雪梨的維多利亞購物中心逛街。
Cecilia: Wow Gracie, I feel like I went back in time at this mall. This is such a quaint place.	西西利雅：哇葛雷絲，我覺得在這個購物中心裡我好像時光倒流回到從前。這真是一個古色古香的地方。
Gracie: Yeah, you're right. This place was built in 1890 as a big	葛雷絲：對啊，你說的沒錯。這個地方是在 1890 年

marketplace, but they kept this historical building and changed it into a fancy shopping center now.

建造的大型市集，但是現在他們保留下來這座歷史建築，然後把它改造成一個高級的購物中心。

Cecilia: There is some amazing marketing strategy going on here. A historical building combining with modern boutiques. Impressive.

西西利雅：這背後有用了很厲害的行銷策略。歷史建築跟現代精品店結合，真不錯。

Grace: Haha...Dear marketing manager, you're on vacation now. Chill, and let's do some shopping!

葛雷絲：哈哈……親愛的行銷經理，你現在在放假。放輕鬆，我們來逛街啦！

Cecilia: Oops, sorry I couldn't help it. That's what happens when you are in the office twenty-four seven brainstorming marketing strategies.

西西利雅：啊呀，不好意思我不是故意的。這就是你二十四小時都在公司裡想著行銷策略的結果。

Grace: It's okay. I was just pick-

葛雷絲：沒關係啦，我只是

ing on you. Although I have to say that the prices here are all on the higher end, so I can take you somewhere else if you are looking for some cheap buys.

在挑你毛病。不過這裡的價格都比較高喔，如果你只是想要找一些比較便宜的東西我也可以帶你去別的地方。

Cecilia: Yeah, it's cool. I don't mind window-shopping. This building is so stunning. Look at the stained glass window and the staircase.

西西利雅：好啊，沒關係。我也很喜歡看看就好。這棟建築物真的好美。你看那個彩色玻璃，還有樓梯。

Gracie: And I love the historical clock there. Did you see that?

葛雷絲：還有我喜歡他們的歷史時鐘。你有看到嗎？

Cecilia: Let's take some pictures of this place. I think I might have some ideas about how we can develop our historical buildings back home.

西西利雅：我們來照點相好了。我有一些點子可以開發我們的歷史建築物。

Gracie: Are you serious? What happens to goodbye work, and

葛雷絲：你是認真的嗎？不是說好不談工作，專心度假

hello vacation?	嗎？
Cecilia: You're right, I'm sorry. Let's go grab a cocktail some-where.	西西利雅：你說的對。對不起。那我們去找個地方喝杯調酒好了。

▶▶ 字彙慣用語補充包

單字	詞性	中譯	單字	詞性	中譯
quaint	*adj.*	古怪的、奇特的	boutique	*n.*	花束
marketplace	*n.*	市場、市集	stunning	*adj.*	驚豔的
fancy	*v.*	喜好、愛好	develop	*v.*	發展

UNIT 22 ▶▶ 荷蘭，烏特勒支 Olivier 的餐廳

▶▶ Dialogue 情境對話 🎧 MP3 34

※現在請跟著 CD 覆誦，練習一整篇完整的對話 shadowing 練習，第一次先跟著 CD 以相同速度覆誦，第二次跟第三次後可以隨個人程度調整並於聽到句子內容後，拉長數秒或更長時間作練習，時間拉的越長，表示能專注聽到的對話訊息內容更多，有助於聽長對話，例如雅思聽力 section 1 和 section 2，以及學術內容即 section 3 和 section 4 的聽力上。

Terence and his friend Denise are going to a restaurant called Olivier in Utrecht.	泰倫斯和他的朋友德尼絲要去在荷蘭烏特勒支，一家叫做 Olivier 的餐廳。
Terence: This is such a neat restaurant Denise! What is this place?	泰倫斯：這家餐廳好酷喔德尼絲！這裡是哪裡啊？
Denise: Impressive, right? It used to be a church and then they renovated this place to a	德尼絲：很棒對吧？這裡以前是一間教堂，然後他們現在把它改造成一間比利時的

Belgian pub. They have a good selection of beers and the food is good, too.

酒吧。這裡有很多啤酒可以選擇，而且食物也很好吃。

Terence: Yeah, it's so spacious, too! They must be doing really good. It's very crowded now.

泰倫斯：對啊，這裡好寬敞喔！他們生意一定很好。現在好多人喔。

Denise: It's always very crowded. I guess that's the only bad thing about this place. You sort of have to yell to talk to each other.

德尼絲：這裡一直都很多人啊！我想這裡唯一不好的地方就是人太多。在這裡講話都要用吼的。

Terence: Nonsense, I think this is fun though. I bet it's really fun to watch any major sports games here.

泰倫斯：胡説，我覺得這樣也很好玩啊！我猜在這看任何重大體育賽事一定很好玩。

Denise: You guessed right! It is always fun to watch sports games here. I came here to watch World Cup here and everyone had a blast.

德尼絲：你猜對了！在這裡看球賽真的很好玩。我上次來這裡看世界盃，超好玩的！

Terence: I bet! Look at the old movies that are projected on the wall, too. I just love the ambience here.

泰倫斯：我想也是！你看牆上投影的那些老電影！我好喜歡這裡的氣氛喔！

Denise: Yeah, you're right. I love the dim light and the decoration. It's very cozy to eat here actually.

德尼絲：你說的對。我很愛他們昏暗的燈光跟擺設。在這吃東西很舒適。

Terence: Very cool Denise. You didn't fail my expectations so far in the Netherland. Well done!

泰倫斯：很酷耶德尼絲。目前為止在荷蘭你還沒讓我失望過！做得好！

Denise: Wait till you try their house-brewed beers. I'll take my full compliment then.

德尼絲：等到你喝過他們自己釀的啤酒你再誇獎我吧我要全套的誇獎！

Terence: Haha...fair enough. Let's order. I can't wait any longer.

泰倫斯：哈哈……好啦。我們來點餐吧。我不能再等下去了。

▶▶ 字彙慣用語補充包

單字	詞性	中譯	單字	詞性	中譯
restaurant	*n.*	餐廳	spacious	*adj.*	寬敞的
renovate	*v.*	翻修	project	*n.*	計畫、企劃
selection	*n.*	選擇	expectation	*n.*	期望

UNIT 23 ▶▶▶ 谷歌虛擬博物館

▶▶ Dialogue 情境對話 🎧 MP3 35

※現在請跟著 CD 覆誦，練習一整篇完整的對話 shadowing 練習，第一次先跟著 CD 以相同速度覆誦，第二次跟第三次後可以隨個人程度調整並於聽到句子內容後，拉長數秒或更長時間作練習，時間拉的越長，表示能專注聽到的對話訊息內容更多，有助於聽長對話，例如雅思聽力 section 1 和 section 2，以及學術內容即 section 3 和 section 4 的聽力上。

Willy and Alice are working in their study at home.	威力和愛麗絲正在他們家的書房工作。
Willy: I can't believe our summer vacation is coming to an end already! I didn't even do the museum visits like I'm supposed to do.	威力：我不敢相信我們的暑假已經要結束了！我都還沒去我應該要去的博物館。
Alice: What do you have to do? Just visit museums? Can't you	愛麗絲：你要去那裡做什麼？只是去參觀博物館嗎？

just look up the information you need on Internet?

你不能上網查一查需要的資料就好了嗎？

Willy: I'm supposed to be there and choose a few art works that I like and want to analyze. But it's too late. I guess your method will have to do.

威力：我應該要去博物館，然後選幾個我喜歡的藝術品然後再分析它們。但是太遲了，我想只好用你的辦法了。

Alice: Wait, I have an idea. You can use the Google Virtual Tours in the Google Cultural Institute! I think they offer up to 17 top museums on line.

愛麗絲：等一下，我有個點子。你可以用谷歌虛擬導覽去谷歌虛擬博物館啊！我想他們在線上有提供十七家頂尖的博物館。

Willy: Wait, what do you mean? I can go to the museums now as long as I'm on-line? Is that what you're implying?

威力：等一下，什麼意思？你說只要我在線上我就可以去博物館嗎？你是想要說這個嗎？

Alice: That's exactly what I'm hinting genius.

愛麗絲：那就是我想說的，天才。

Willy: How though? I mean it sounds great, but how did they do it?

威力：但是怎麼可以？我是說聽起來很棒，可是他們怎麼做到的？

Alice: Simple! They use the Street View technology they do with a Google Map, but then this time they make it into a virtual tour!

愛麗絲：很簡單啊！他們是用谷歌地圖街景的技術，但是這次他們把它做成虛擬導覽。

Willy: That's so tight! Have you tried it yet?

威力：超酷的！你有試過了嗎？

Alice: Neh, I just heard it from my art professor.

愛麗絲：還沒，我是聽我藝術課的教授説的。

Willy: Guess who's going to the museum with me?

威力：你猜猜看誰要陪我去博物館啊？

Alice: Oh, Willy, I have my work to do as well! Why don't you help mine once you're done

愛麗絲：喔威力！我也有作業要做啊！你幹嘛不導覽完你的博物館之後來幫我。

with the museum tour!

Willy: Okay, but thanks for the great info! Nice save sis!

威力：好啦，但是謝謝你跟我說這個資訊啊！救得好啊妹妹！

▶▶ 字彙慣用語補充包

單字	詞性	中譯	單字	詞性	中譯
museum	*n.*	博物館	analyze	*v.*	分析
information	*n.*	資訊	method	*n.*	方法
choose	*v.*	選擇	hint	*v.*	暗示

UNIT 24 ▶▶ 義大利的比薩斜塔

▶▶ Dialogue 情境對話 🎧 MP3 36

※現在請跟著 CD 覆誦，練習一整篇完整的對話 shadowing 練習，第一次先跟著 CD 以相同速度覆誦，第二次跟第三次後可以隨個人程度調整並於聽到句子內容後，拉長數秒或更長時間作練習，時間拉的越長，表示能專注聽到的對話訊息內容更多，有助於聽長對話，例如雅思聽力 section 1 和 section 2，以及學術內容即 section 3 和 section 4 的聽力上。

Julia and Kate are at the Leaning Tower of Pisa in Italy.	朱麗雅和凱特正在義大利的比薩斜塔。
Julia: We're finally here!!! That's the Leaning Tower of Pisa!	朱麗雅：我們終於到了！那就是比薩斜塔耶！
Kate: The architecture here is gorgeous. Should we take a few selfies with the tower?	凱特：這裡的建築物都好美喔。我們要不要也來跟這個塔自拍一下？

聽力『講解』

聽力『演練』

聽力『實戰』

口說『演練+實戰』

Julia: Hahaha...that man looks like he's pooping the tower. So creative. I'm just gonna pretend I'm pushing it back!

朱麗雅：哈哈哈……那個男的好像在拍他正在把比薩斜塔大出來。好有創意喔。我要來假裝我把它推回去就好了！

Kate: hahaha okay! Got it! Should we go get the tickets to get the tower now?

凱特：哈哈哈好啊！好拍到了！我們要不要去買票進去？

Julia: Yeah, what do you think? To go to other buildings are all five euros, but to climb up the Leaning Tower of Pisa costs seventeen euros!

朱麗雅：好啊，你覺得呢？進去其他建築物是五歐元，可是要進去爬比薩斜塔要十七歐元！

Kate: What a rip off! But we are here already. We might as well go!

凱特：真是敲竹槓！但是我們已經在這了。我們可以去一下啦！

Julia: You're right. We've made it this far. Okay, let's go get the tickets then.

朱麗雅：你說的對！我們都從這麼遠來了。好吧，我們去買票吧。

(After they got their tickets) （在他們買到票之後）

Julia: It feels so weird to climb in a tower that's tilted.

朱麗雅：我覺得在斜塔裡面往上爬好奇怪噢。

Kate: And it's spiral stairs here. I'm getting dizzy.

凱特：而且這裡還是旋轉樓梯。我開始頭暈了。

Julia: Me, too. There are 293 steps in total. We can do this! Come on Kate!

朱麗雅：我也是。總共有兩百九十三階。我們可以的！加油凱特！

Kate: Why did we pay seventeen euros to go through this ordeal?

凱特：我們為什麼要付十七歐元來經歷這災難？

Julia: It will be worth it. Let's take a break and take some pictures!

朱麗雅：很值得的啦！我們休息一下跟拍些照好了！

Kate: Sounds great to me! I feel

凱特：好啊！我覺得我好像

	中文
like an old lady.	老太婆喔。
Julia: Water, grandma?	朱麗雅：你要喝水嗎，阿嬤？

▶▶ 字彙慣用語補充包

單字	詞性	中譯	單字	詞性	中譯
architecture	*n.*	建築	pretend	*v.*	假裝
gorgeous	*adj.*	華麗的	building	*n.*	建築
creative	*adj.*	創意的	dizzy	*adj.*	暈眩的

UNIT 25 ▶▶ 荷蘭騎自行車

▶▶ Dialogue 情境對話 🎧 MP3 37

※現在請跟著 CD 覆誦，練習一整篇完整的對話 shadowing 練習，
第一次先跟著 CD 以相同速度覆誦，第二次跟第三次後可以隨個人
程度調整並於聽到句子內容後，拉長數秒或更長時間作練習，時
間拉的越長，表示能專注聽到的對話訊息內容更多，有助於聽長
對話，例如雅思聽力 section 1 和 section 2，以及學術內容即
section 3 和 section 4 的聽力上。

Jay is renting a bike from a bike shop from the clerk Meredith in the Netherlands.	杰正在荷蘭的一家腳踏車店裡跟店員梅若迪絲租腳踏車。
Jay: Hi, So I'm going to take this one for 3 days.	杰：嗨，我要租這台三天。
Meredith: Okay no problem, so just be sure to take it back by noon on the fourth day.	梅若迪絲：好啊，沒問題，所以第四天中午之前帶腳踏車回來就可以了。

Jay: Okay, oh and another thing is that I heard the bike theft here is pretty bad. Do you mind if I pick your brains for any tips of where to park and all that?

杰：好，喔還有就是我聽說這裡腳踏車偷竊案很多。你介不介意我請教你關於要停在哪裡那類的問題？

Meredith: It is bad, but usually if you lock your bike along with all the other bikes, you should be fine. At least you're not the only one on the menu. You know what I mean? However, we do have a policy that if you lost the bike, you have to purchase it.

梅若迪絲：偷竊案是真的蠻多的，但是通常如果你把你的腳踏車和其他車鎖在相同地方，其實應該還好。至少你不是偷竊案名單上唯一的一個。你懂我的意思嗎？但是我們有一個政策是如果你遺失了腳踏車，那你就要買下它。

Jay: Yes, I understand that. But I would love it if that doesn't happen, so there's really nothing to look out for?

杰：嗯，我知道。但是當然我希望最好是不會發生啦，所以真得沒有什麼是要注意的嗎？

Meredith: For your information, here's the area you want to stay away from (circling on the map)

梅若迪絲：這裡是你應該要知道的，你應該要遠離這一區（在地圖上圈起），然後

and I can give you an extra lock if that makes you feel better?

我可以給你額外的鎖，如果這樣會讓你放心一點。

Jay: Yeah sure, thanks so much. I would hate it if something bad happens to your bike, too.

杰：好的謝謝你。如果你們的腳踏車出了甚麼事，我也是真的會很難過。

Meredith: You will be fine. Don't worry. So now that's out of the way, let me show you the fun area of this city!

梅若迪絲：不會有事發生的。別擔心。所以現在那個處理好了，讓我來跟你説這個城市哪裡好玩吧！

▶▶ 字彙慣用語補充包

單字	詞性	中譯	單字	詞性	中譯
rent	*v.*	租	menu	*n.*	菜單
Netherland	*n.*	荷蘭	circle	*n.*	圈
usually	*adj.*	通常	happen	*v.*	發生

UNIT 26 ▶▶ 巴塞隆納的青年旅社

▶▶ Dialogue 情境對話 🎧 MP3 38

※現在請跟著 CD 覆誦，練習一整篇完整的對話 shadowing 練習，第一次先跟著 CD 以相同速度覆誦，第二次跟第三次後可以隨個人程度調整並於聽到句子內容後，拉長數秒或更長時間作練習，時間拉的越長，表示能專注聽到的對話訊息內容更多，有助於聽長對話，例如雅思聽力 section 1 和 section 2，以及學術內容即 section 3 和 section 4 的聽力上。

Paul is checking in a hostel in Barcelona.	保羅正在巴塞隆納的一間青年旅社登記入住。
Paul: Hola, I have a reservation under Paul Brown.	保羅：嗨（西文），我有用保羅柏朗這個名字訂了一間房間。
Anna the clerk: Hola Paul, my name is Anna! Can I see your passport?	安娜（櫃檯）：嗨（西文）保羅，我叫安娜！我可以看一下你的護照嗎？

Paul: Sure, here you are. Sorry to come in so late.

保羅：當然可以，在這裡。不好意思這麼晚才來。

Anna: No problem. We have a lot of visitors coming in at this time, too. Is this your first time in Barcelona?

安娜：沒關係。我們有很多遊客也是這時候才來。這是你第一次來巴塞隆納嗎？

Paul: Yeah, it is my first time. I'm very excited!

保羅：對啊，這是我第一次來。我很興奮耶！

Anna: Oh great! Welcome! I'll give you a map and some suggestions. Let me show you around at the lounge area and the computer area. We have Wifi, too, if you need it for your phone or other devices.

Anna: 喔太好了！歡迎！我會給你一張地圖跟一些建議。讓我帶你看一下我們的休息區和電腦區。如果你的電話還是其他設備需要的話，我們也有 wifi 喔！

Paul: Great, thank you so much! Wow, there are still many people here at this hour.

保羅：太好了！謝謝你！哇，這麼晚了還有這麼多人在這裡。

聽力『講解』

聽力『演練』

聽力『實戰』

口說『演練＋實戰』

Anna: Yes, this group had just come in before you. They are going to a local tapas bar if you want to join them!

安娜：對啊，這群人也是在你來之前才剛到的。如果你想加入他們的話，他們要去一間當地的西班牙小酒吧喔！

Paul: Yes, that will be wonderful to meet some friends I think. Thanks for the tips and I will try and ask if I can join them to the tapas bar.

保羅：喔好阿，我想交一些新朋友也不錯！謝謝你的提醒，還有我會去問他們我可以不可以加入！

Anna: We have breakfast here at 8 a.m. if you would like to eat, and we have a few historical walking tours at 10 am if you care to join tomorrow morning.

安娜：如果你想吃東西的話，我們早上八點有早餐，然後明早十點會有幾個歷史的徒步行程，如果你想加入的話。

Paul: Thanks Anna for all your help!

保羅：謝謝你的幫忙安娜！

▶▶ 字彙慣用語補充包

單字	詞性	中譯	單字	詞性	中譯
reservation	*n.*	訂位	suggestion	*n.*	建議
passport	*n.*	護照	lounge	*n.*	休息區
visitor	*n.*	參訪者	historical	*adj.*	歷史的

聽力『講解』

聽力『演練』

聽力『實戰』

口說『演練＋實戰』

UNIT 27 ▶▶ 印度的機場

▶▶ Dialogue 情境對話 🎧 MP3 39

※現在請跟著 CD 覆誦，練習一整篇完整的對話 shadowing 練習，第一次先跟著 CD 以相同速度覆誦，第二次跟第三次後可以隨個人程度調整並於聽到句子內容後，拉長數秒或更長時間作練習，時間拉的越長，表示能專注聽到的對話訊息內容更多，有助於聽長對話，例如雅思聽力 section 1 和 section 2，以及學術內容即 section 3 和 section 4 的聽力上。

Robert is taking a taxi from the airport to his hotel in India. His driver is Tilak.	羅柏正在印度的機場搭了一臺計程車要到他的飯店。他的司機的名字是提拉克。
Tilak: Good morning sir, my name is Tilak. Where do you want to go?	提拉克:早安，先生。我的名字是提拉克。你想要去哪裡呢？
Robert: Please take me to the Hilton New Delhi Hotel.	羅柏：請帶我到希爾頓新德里飯店。

Tilak: No problem, sir.

提拉克：沒問題，先生。

Robert: Wow, be careful Tilak. The traffic is pretty bad here, right?

羅柏：哇，小心啊提拉克！這裡的交通蠻差的喔？

Tilak: Yes, sir. There is always a lot going on here.

提拉克：對啊，先生。路上總是蠻多狀況的。

Robert: Are those cows in the middle of the road?

羅柏：在路中間的那些是牛嗎？

Tilak: Yes, sir. They are very holy animals, so we cannot shush them away.

提拉克：是的先生。牠們是非常神聖的動物，所以我們不可以噓牠們走。

Robert: Watch out!!! There is someone running across the street. How can you drive here? There is so much going on on the road. Cars, Tuk Tuks, bikes, pedestrians, cows...

羅柏：小心！！！有人剛跑過馬路。你怎麼有辦法在這裡開車？路上真的太多狀況了！車子，嘟嘟車，腳踏車，行人，牛…

Tilak: You'll get used to it after a while.

提拉克：你過一陣子就會習慣了。

Robert: I can understand why everyone is honking constantly now.

羅柏：我現在可以了解為什麼大家都一直按喇叭了！

Tilak: Yeah, it's a way to communicate, but mostly to tell people to get away!

提拉克：對啊，那其實是溝通的一種辦法，但是大部分的時間我們是在説讓開！

Robert: I see. I also realize something else that's interesting.

羅柏：我懂。我也發現還有另一件事情蠻有趣的。

Tilak: What is that sir?

提拉克：是什麼事呢先生？

Rober: Your driver's seat is on the left, and you drive on the left as well. In my country, our driver's seat is on the left, but we drive on the right side of the road.

羅柏：你們的駕駛座是在左邊，而且你們也是開在路的左邊。在我的國家，我們的駕駛座是在左邊，但是我們開車是開在路的右邊。

聽力『講解』

聽力『演練』

聽力『實戰』

口說『演練+實戰』

Tilak: Oh...no sir. We "should" drive on the right side of the road technically...

提拉克：喔……不是的先生。我們其實「應該要」開在路的右邊啦……

▶▶ 字彙慣用語補充包

單字	詞性	中譯	單字	詞性	中譯
honk	*v.*	按喇叭	interesting	*adj.*	令人感到興趣的
constantly	*adj.*	不斷地	country	*n.*	國家
communicate	*v.*	溝通	technically	*adv.*	技術性地

UNIT 28 ▶▶ 印度的飯店

▶▶ Dialogue 情境對話 🎧 MP3 40

※現在請跟著 CD 覆誦，練習一整篇完整的對話 shadowing 練習，第一次先跟著 CD 以相同速度覆誦，第二次跟第三次後可以隨個人程度調整並於聽到句子內容後，拉長數秒或更長時間作練習，時間拉的越長，表示能專注聽到的對話訊息內容更多，有助於聽長對話，例如雅思聽力 section 1 和 section 2，以及學術內容即 section 3 和 section 4 的聽力上。

Amanda and Michael are checking in a hotel in India when she found out that she lost her passport.	艾曼達和麥可正要在印度的一家飯店登記入住，可是艾曼達發現她的護照不見了。
Amanda: Just a second. Sorry, I have so much stuff in my bag, and I will never find anything in this bag.	艾曼達：等一下喔。對不起我有好多東西在我的包包裡。在這包包裡我永遠都找不到任何東西。
Michael: Haha...That's okay, as	麥可：哈哈……沒關係，只

long as you find the passport. It is just a little important. We have to leave for Bali tomorrow.

要你找得到你的護照就好了。這只有一點點的重要。我們明天就要飛峇里島了。

Amanda: Yeah, I know, Michael. You were not helping...Hang on. I think I really lost my passport this time.

艾曼達：對啊，我知道。麥可，你沒有幫到忙喔……等等。我覺得我這次好像真的弄丟我的護照了。

Michael: Stop joking around. Come on Amanda. Let's check in and go explore the city a little bit.

麥可：不要再開玩笑了啦！艾曼達快點啦，我們趕快登記然後去看看這個城市。

Amanda: For once I'm not joking. I've looked everywhere. Help me out here Michael. I need your help.

艾曼達：我第一次沒在開玩笑。我到處都找過了。幫我找啦麥可。我需要你的幫忙！

Michael: Cut it out Amanda! This is really not funny...Are you serious? What? Give me your bag.

麥可：不要鬧了艾曼達！一點都不好玩……你是認真的嗎？什麼？給我你的包包。

171

(After both of them going through all Amanda's bags)

（在他們兩個都找遍了艾曼達的包包後）

Amanda: What should I do? Our flight is tomorrow. I'm so sorry Michael. If anything, go without me, and I'll find my way there.

艾曼達：我該怎麼辦？我們是搭明天的飛機耶。對不起啦麥可。不過萬一沒辦法的話，你就先走，我會再想辦法過去。

Michael: Don't be silly. I'm sure there's an American Embassy here. Let's call them and see what the options are. I'm sure this happens all the time.

麥可：別傻了。這裡一定有美國大使館。我們打電話給他們問問看我們該怎麼做。這一定常常發生。

Amanda: That people lost their passports? I'm such a mess. Michael, I'm so sorry.

艾曼達：你說大家丟掉護照常常發生嗎？我真是一團亂耶。麥可，對不起啦。

Michael: Don't worry about it. Now let's move on and fix it together. It's not the end of the world, come on.

麥可：別擔心了啦。現在我們一起去把事情解決，這又不是世界末日，拜託。

Amanda: What did I do to deserve you?

艾曼達：我到底燒了什麼好香可以有你在我身邊？

Michael: You cook well.

麥可：你煮飯很好吃。

▶▶ 字彙慣用語補充包

單字	詞性	中譯	單字	詞性	中譯
explore	*v.*	探索	option	*n.*	選擇
flight	*n.*	飛行、飛機的班次	fix	*v.*	修理
embassy	*n.*	大使館	deserve	*v.*	應受、該得

UNIT 29 ▶▶ 聖安東尼奧

▶▶ Dialogue 情境對話 🎧 MP3 41

※現在請跟著 CD 覆誦，練習一整篇完整的對話 shadowing 練習，第一次先跟著 CD 以相同速度覆誦，第二次跟第三次後可以隨個人程度調整並於聽到句子內容後，拉長數秒或更長時間作練習，時間拉的越長，表示能專注聽到的對話訊息內容更多，有助於聽長對話，例如雅思聽力 section 1 和 section 2，以及學術內容即 section 3 和 section 4 的聽力上。

Alex and Jasmine are getting on a boat ride at the River walk at San Antonio.	艾力克斯和潔斯敏正在聖安東尼奧河濱的游船上。
Jasmine: This is such a romantic experience. Thanks Alex!	潔斯敏：這真是一個浪漫的體驗。謝謝你艾力克斯！
Alex: You're welcome. I think you definitely made a good call on coming here after Thanksgiving. Look at the lights around	艾力克斯：不客氣。我想你做了很好的決定説要感恩節過後再來。你看我們周遭的燈！

聽力『講解』

聽力『演練』

聽力『實戰』

口説『演練+實戰』

us.

Jasmine: This is very touristy, but I love it. I'm not going to forget any of this.

潔斯敏：我知道這很像個觀光客，但是我超愛的。我一定不會忘記這一切的。

Alex: I'm glad you enjoy it! It is our 2nd anniversary after all.

艾力克斯：我很開心你很喜歡！這畢竟是我們結婚兩週年紀念。

Jasmine: People are waving at us from the shore!

潔斯敏：有人在岸上跟我們揮手耶！

Alex: Wave back! I'm videotaping all this!

艾力克斯：揮回去啊！我正在錄影！

Jasmine: I'm not sure whether it is the wine or the beautiful lights. I'm euphoric.

潔斯敏：我不確定是因為酒還是這美麗的燈。我好興奮。

Alex: I feel so happy as well. I'm

艾力克斯：我也覺得好開

glad we came out here.

心。我好高興我們來這。

Jasmine: Should we get some dinner here as well? I'm in love with this side of the city.

潔斯敏：我們要不要也在這裡吃晚餐？我好喜歡這個城市的這個角落。

Alex: Don't you worry, my darling, I've made a reservation at one Mexican restaurant already.

艾力克斯：你不必擔心，親愛的。我已經在這裡的一間墨西哥餐廳訂好位。

Jasmine: Thank you so much. I married the most thoughtful man on earth.

潔斯敏：真的謝謝你。我嫁給了全地球最體貼的男人。

Alex: The boat ride is about 40 minutes long, so we should be hungry by then. We will have to celebrate afterwards!

艾力克斯：這個游船行程大概四十分鐘，所以我們結束後應該也餓了。我們等等一定要慶祝一下！

Jasmine: Yes, and let's come down here every year!

潔斯敏：好！我們每年都來這裡吧！

▶▶ 字彙慣用語補充包

單字	詞性	中譯	單字	詞性	中譯
anniversary	*n.*	周年紀念	thoughtful	*adj.*	體貼的
wave	*v.*	揮舞	hungry	*adj.*	飢餓的
euphoric	*adj.*	心情愉快、心滿意足的	celebrate	*v.*	慶祝

UNIT 30 ▶▶ 太平洋屋脊步道

▶▶ Dialogue 情境對話 🎧 MP3 42

※現在請跟著 CD 覆誦，練習一整篇完整的對話 shadowing 練習，第一次先跟著 CD 以相同速度覆誦，第二次跟第三次後可以隨個人程度調整並於聽到句子內容後，拉長數秒或更長時間作練習，時間拉的越長，表示能專注聽到的對話訊息內容更多，有助於聽長對話，例如雅思聽力 section 1 和 section 2，以及學術內容即 section 3 和 section 4 的聽力上。

Brandon and Erin ran into each other in the Pacific Crest Trail together.	布蘭登和艾琳在太平洋屋脊步道遇到彼此。
Brandon: How are you doing so far?	布蘭登：你目前為止怎麼樣？
Erin: I'm doing good. I just wish I packed lighter for this trip.	艾琳：我很好。我只希望我當初來的時候打包輕一點。

Brandon: How far are you going to hike?

布蘭登：你要健行多遠呢？

Erin: I'm just trying not to quit every day. My goal is to stay in here for a month.

艾琳：我現在每天只希望我不要放棄。我的目標是在這裡待一個月。

Brandon: That's neat! I'm trying to finish the trail.

布蘭登：好棒！我要把整個步道走完！

Erin: Wow, the whole thing? How long have you been here?

艾琳：哇，整個步道？你在這裡多久了？

Brandon: I have been here for 2 months already. I'm enjoying every bit of it.

布蘭登：我已經在這裡兩個月了。我很享受每一個部分。

Erin: Have you seen any wildlife yet?

艾琳：你有看到任何野生動物了嗎？

Brandon: Plenty. I saw bears

布蘭登：很多。我上禮拜看

last week. They are such gorgeous animals.

到熊。他們真是令人驚艷的動物。

Erin: Wow, weren't you scared?

艾琳：哇，你不怕嗎？

Brandon: Not too much. I made some noises the whole way, so I guess they knew I was coming. They were not too close to me, but enough for me to appreciate their beauty.

布蘭登：不太怕。我整路都有在發出一點噪音，所以我想他們知道我來了。他們沒有很靠近我，但是還是在我可以欣賞他們的美的距離。

Erin: Wow, that sounds pretty amazing! What kind of noises were you making? I saw quite a few deers the other day as well.

艾琳：哇，聽起來好棒噢！你是在製造什麼噪音呢？我前幾天也有看到幾隻鹿。

Brandon: I was mostly talking to myself. You have no idea how happy I am to run into you!

布蘭登：我大部分都是在跟我自己説話。你不知道遇到你我有多開心！

Erin: I have seen your name for

艾琳：其實我已經看到你的

a long time, and have been try-ing to catch up with you. Sorry it took me so long. | 名字很久了，而且一直想要追趕上你。對不起花了這麼久才追上你。

Brandon: Haha, better late than never! | 布蘭登：哈哈，遲到總比沒來好！

▶▶ 字彙慣用語補充包

單字	詞性	中譯	單字	詞性	中譯
pack	*v.*	包裹	gorgeous	*adj.*	華麗的
goal	*n.*	目標	enjoy	*v.*	享受
wildlife	*n.*	野生動物	appreciate	*v.*	欣賞

UNIT 31 ▶▶ 秘魯的傳統食物

▶▶ Dialogue 情境對話 🎧 MP3 43

※現在請跟著 CD 覆誦，練習一整篇完整的對話 shadowing 練習，
第一次先跟著 CD 以相同速度覆誦，第二次跟第三次後可以隨個人
程度調整並於聽到句子內容後，拉長數秒或更長時間作練習，時
間拉的越長，表示能專注聽到的對話訊息內容更多，有助於聽長
對話，例如雅思聽力 section 1 和 section 2，以及學術內容即
section 3 和 section 4 的聽力上。

Dennis and April are going to try the traditional food in Peru.	丹尼斯和艾波正要試吃秘魯的傳統食物。
Dennis: What should we order? Ceviche?	丹尼斯：我們要點什麼呢？Ceviche？
April: What exactly is a Ceviche again?	艾波：Ceviche 到底是什麼？
Dennis: It's basically raw sea-	丹尼斯：其實就是生海鮮和

food with citrus juice.

酸橘汁。

April: Sounds like food poison!

艾波：聽起來像是食物中毒！

Dennis: No, it does not, the acid from the citrus juice will cook the raw meat. It's good. Let's give it a try.

丹尼斯：才不會，酸橘汁中的酸會把生肉煮熟。很好吃！我們試試看！

April: Look at this one "Cuy". Did I read it correctly? Traditional roasted guinea pig?

艾波：你看這個「Cuy」。我剛剛有讀錯嗎？傳統的烤天竺鼠？

Dennis: Oh yeah, it is actually one of the main dishes here.

丹尼斯：噢對，那其實是這裡的主菜之一。

April: What? Aren't guinea pigs pets? And they are some sorts of rodents, right?

艾波：什麼？天竺鼠不是寵物嗎？而且牠們是不是鼠類的一種嗎？

Dennis: Well...if you want to put it that way...

丹尼斯：恩……如果你要那麼說的話……

April: No, I don't want to eat rats. Next.

艾波：不要，我不要吃老鼠。下一個。

Dennis: Hey we have to try it. You can't find this dish anywhere else! We're getting it!

丹尼斯：嘿，我們要試試看。你在別的地方找不到的！我們要點這個！

April: What? I refuse to eat it.

艾波：什麼？我拒絕吃這道。

Dennis: That's okay. Just for the sake of it. We'll order and see what we think!

丹尼斯：沒關係。就試試看。我們點了再看我們到時候覺得怎麼樣！

April: You can't trick me into eating it. I'm not falling for this one.

艾波：你這次騙不了我吃這個。我這次不會上當。

Dennis: It will be a memorable experience.	丹尼斯：這會是一個難忘的經驗。
April: Can I have a big bowl of rice and a big bottle of beer then, please!!	艾波：那我可以點一大碗白飯和一大瓶啤酒嗎，拜託！！
Dennis: You got it!!	丹尼斯：沒問題！！

▶▶ 字彙慣用語補充包

單字	詞性	中譯	單字	詞性	中譯
basically	*adv.*	基本地	acid	*n.*	酸
seafood	*n.*	海鮮	traditional	*adj.*	傳統的
poison	*n.*	毒藥	refuse	*v.*	拒絕

UNIT 32 ▶▶ 紐奧良 狂歡節

▶▶ Dialogue 情境對話 🎧 MP3 44

※現在請跟著 CD 覆誦，練習一整篇完整的對話 shadowing 練習，第一次先跟著 CD 以相同速度覆誦，第二次跟第三次後可以隨個人程度調整並於聽到句子內容後，拉長數秒或更長時間作練習，時間拉的越長，表示能專注聽到的對話訊息內容更多，有助於聽長對話，例如雅思聽力 section 1 和 section 2，以及學術內容即 section 3 和 section 4 的聽力上。

Charles and Patty are going to Mardi Gras.	查爾斯和佩蒂要去參加狂歡節活動。
Patty: How do I look? Look at the beads and the mask I made last night!	佩蒂：我看起來怎麼樣？看看我昨晚做的這些串珠和面具！
Charles: You look amazing! Nice outfit Patty! I just bought the mask this morning at the store!	查爾斯：你看起來棒透了！很棒的服裝佩蒂！我只有今天早上在店裡買的面具！

Patty: That will do! I should know this...but what does Mardi Gras mean anyways?

佩蒂：那也可以啊！我應該知道這個的……但是狂歡節到底是什麼意思？

Charles: It is actually a festival from France. Mardi Gras means Fat Tuesday in English.

查爾斯：這其實是來自法國的節慶。狂歡節到底是什麼意思？在英文是肥膩星期二的意思。

Patty: Fat Tuesday? How come?

佩蒂：肥膩星期二？為什麼？

Charles: They usually have a big celebration before their fast, so before the Ash Wednesday, they have the fat Tuesday. They will eat lots on this day.

查爾斯：他們通常在齋戒之前都會有一場很大的慶祝活動，所以在聖灰星期三前，他們會有肥膩星期二。他們通常會在這天吃很多。

Patty: Are we going to eat lots later? Is that what's gonna happen?

佩蒂：我們等一下也會吃很多嗎？這是等一下會發生的事嗎？

Charles: You can. But eating lots

查爾斯：可以啊。可是在這

on Mardi Gras was the original idea. To have a feast before they started a fast. However, it became a big festival through time. Now people have parades, and all sorts of celebration.

天吃很多是最一開始的意思。在開始禁食前有一個大餐。可是現在已經演變為一個很大的慶典。現在人們有遊行，還有各式各樣的慶祝活動。

Patty: Wow, that sounds fun! Thanks Charles.

佩蒂：哇，聽起來真好玩！謝啦查爾斯。

Charles: You're welcome!

查爾斯：不客氣！

Patty: So I guess we should head to the French Quarter for the parade now, right?

佩蒂：所以我們應該要去法國區看遊行隊吧？

Charles: Yes, unless you want to eat lots now! Haha.

查爾斯：對啊，除非你想要先大吃！哈哈。

Patty: Hey that's not a bad idea, either! Let it be the real fat Tuesday!

佩蒂：嘿！那也是一個很好的主意啊！就讓今天成為真正的肥膩星期二吧！

▶▶ 字彙慣用語補充包

單字	詞性	中譯	單字	詞性	中譯
bead	*n.*	珠子	celebration	*n.*	慶祝
outfit	*n.*	配備	original	*adj.*	原始的
festival	*n.*	節慶	parade	*n.*	遊行

UNIT 33 ▶▶ 伊斯坦堡咖啡廳

▶▶ Dialogue 情境對話 🎧 MP3 45

※現在請跟著 CD 覆誦，練習一整篇完整的對話 shadowing 練習，第一次先跟著 CD 以相同速度覆誦，第二次跟第三次後可以隨個人程度調整並於聽到句子內容後，拉長數秒或更長時間作練習，時間拉的越長，表示能專注聽到的對話訊息內容更多，有助於聽長對話，例如雅思聽力 section 1 和 section 2，以及學術內容即 section 3 和 section 4 的聽力上。

Rebecca and her local friend Cansin are at a local coffee house.	瑞貝卡和她當地的朋友坎欣正在當地的一家咖啡廳裡。
Rebecca: Wow this is so nice. There are coffee houses everywhere here.	瑞貝卡：哇這裡好棒喔。到處都有咖啡廳。
Cansin: Yes, we love to drink coffee. It's just a nice place to hang out with friends or enjoy a book to yourself you know.	坎欣：對啊，我們很愛喝咖啡。這就是一個和朋友見面或是自己來這邊讀一本書很棒的地方。

Rebecca: That's so cool. The coffee seems so thick here. I can see the sediments at the bottom of the cup.

瑞貝卡：好酷喔。這裡的咖啡感覺好濃喔。我可以看到杯底的沉澱物。

Cansin: Yeah, we grind the coffee into very fine powders that's why. You can really taste the real coffee flavor that way. It's quite strong though. I have to warn you. I can tell your fortune by reading the coffee grinds. Do you want to try?

坎欣：對啊，那是因為我們把咖啡磨得很細。那樣你才可以品嚐到咖啡真正的風味。那還蠻濃的喔，我必須先警告你。我還可以從咖啡渣來算你的命喔。你想要試試看嗎？

Rebecca: A coffee grind fortune telling? Yes, please!

瑞貝卡：咖啡渣算命？好，拜託！

Cansin: Okay, so first drink the coffee and leave the grind behind.

坎欣：好，那首先你先喝咖啡，然後把咖啡渣留下。

(Rebecca sips the coffee)

（瑞貝卡啜飲咖啡）

Rebecca: Okay. Done! Wow, it is quite strong.

瑞貝卡：好，喝完了！哇，真的很濃。

Cansin: Then make a wish before you cover the coffee cup with the dish.

坎欣：然後在你把杯蓋放在咖啡杯上之前許個願望。

Rebecca: Okay.

瑞貝卡：好了。

Cansin: Alright. Gently flip the cup upside down. And now we wait till the grind to settle and dry.

坎欣：好，現在輕輕地把杯子整個翻過來。然後我們現在要等到咖啡渣沈澱和乾掉。

(10 minutes later)

（十分鐘過後）

Cansin: Okay, let's see what we have here. I see a circle, which means everything is going well, and your wish is most likely to come true.

坎欣：好，讓我們來看看我們有什麼。我看到一個圈圈，意思是說每一件事情都很順利，而且你的願望很有可能會實現。

Rebecca: Hooray! What else does it say?

瑞貝卡：萬歲！它還說了什麼？

Cansin: Oh no...

坎欣：噢不⋯⋯

Rebecca: What?

瑞貝卡：怎麼了？

Cansin: It also says that you will lose some money. Cansin forgot to bring her wallet, so you might have to pay for her first...

坎欣：他説你會破財。坎欣沒帶錢包所以你要先幫她付錢⋯⋯

Rebecca: Really?? That's no problem. But will you tell me more first before I pay?

瑞貝卡：真的嗎？那沒問題。可是你可以在我付錢之前先告訴我多一點嗎？

▶▶ 字彙慣用語補充包

單字	詞性	中譯	單字	詞性	中譯
sediments	*n.*	沉澱物	flavor	*n.*	風味
grind	*v.*	研磨	fortune	*n.*	命運
taste	*v.*	品嚐	wallet	*n.*	皮包

UNIT 34 ▶▶ 可愛島 Napali 沿岸划輕型獨木舟

▶▶ Dialogue 情境對話 MP3 46

※現在請跟著 CD 覆誦，練習一整篇完整的對話 shadowing 練習，第一次先跟著 CD 以相同速度覆誦，第二次跟第三次後可以隨個人程度調整並於聽到句子內容後，拉長數秒或更長時間作練習，時間拉的越長，表示能專注聽到的對話訊息內容更多，有助於聽長對話，例如雅思聽力 section 1 和 section 2，以及學術內容即 section 3 和 section 4 的聽力上。

Tammy and Matt decided to kayak along Napali coast.	譚咪和麥特決定要沿著 Napali 沿岸划輕型獨木舟。
Tammy: Wow, this is absolutely mind blowing!	譚咪：哇，這真是太令人興奮了！
Matt: Yeah, It's such a beautiful day today, too. The water is so glassy.	麥特：對啊，今天也真是美麗的一天。海水像玻璃般光滑。

Tammy: Yeah, this is such a great idea Matt! Sorry, I was chickened out on the Kalaulau trail!

譚咪：對啊，這真是一個好主意麥特！對不起我因為害怕而沒去 Kalaulau 步道！

Matt: Not a problem at all. This is not too bad, either. We can still make it to the Kalaulau beach this way!

麥特：沒關係。這裡也不差啊。我們這樣還是可以去到 Kalaulau 海邊！

Tammy: I hope so!

譚咪：希望如此！

Matt: We can do it. We just have to keep an eye on our position. We don't want to drift too far from the shore.

麥特：我們可以做到的。我們只是要留心注意我們的位置。我們不想要漂到離岸邊太遠的地方。

Tammy: No, that does not sound fun at all. Luckily, it's not too windy today!

譚咪：不，那一點也不好玩。幸運的是今天風沒有很大！

Matt: No. We are very lucky! Wait!! Do you see the fin that's

麥特：沒錯。我們真的很幸運！等等！！你有看到朝我

swimming towards us?	們游過來的魚鰭嗎？
Tammy: What?! Don't scare me! Is it a shark?	譚咪：什麼？！不要嚇我！是鯊魚嗎？
Matt: I am not sure! Keep your hands in the kayak!	麥特：我不確定！你的手不要超出獨木舟！
Tammy: What?! What can we do besides that?	譚咪：什麼？！除了那個我們還能做什麼？
Matt: Whatever you do, don't jump off this kayak!	麥特：不管你做什麼，千萬別跳下這獨木舟！
Tammy: Why would I do that?	譚咪：為什麼我會想要那樣做？
Tammy: Matt?	譚咪：麥特？
Matt: Wait a second...	麥特：等等……

Tammy: Talk to me Matt, I'm freaking out!	譚咪：現在是什麼狀況麥特，我快嚇死了！
Matt: I think...	麥特：我想……
Tammy: What are you thinking? This is driving me nuts!	譚咪：你在想什麼？這快把我逼瘋了！
Matt: I think they are a pod of dolphins, Tammy! This is amazing!	麥特：我想這是一群海豚，譚咪！這真是太神奇了！
Tammy: What? Really? Where's our GoPro??	譚咪：什麼？真的嗎？我們的 GoPro 攝影機呢？

聽力「講解」
聽力「演練」
聽力「實戰」
口說「演練＋實戰」

▶▶ 字彙慣用語補充包

單字	詞性	中譯	單字	詞性	中譯
absolutely	*adv.*	絕對地	glassy	*adj.*	玻璃似的、光滑的
mind	*n.*	心智、頭腦、智力	position	*n.*	位置
blowing	*adj.*	吹動的	dolphin	*n.*	海豚

Part **2**
雅思口說篇

篇章概述

雅思口説常會需要許多生活經驗作輔助，才能在考場中回答不打結，且傳達出更 believable 的訊息，進而打動考官。這個篇章收錄了 30 個精彩主題，每個回答都道地且活潑，從單句口説做練習，進而拓展成一氣呵成講完一段敘述，最後融合自己本身答案獲取高分。

（小提點：想拿高分……就別再背模板囉……一緊張可能還忘了要講什麼喔！）

UNIT 1 ▶▶ 瀑布

▶▶ 單句口說

1. Niagara Falls is my favorite waterfalls.

   尼加拉瀑布是我最喜歡的瀑布。

   字彙輔助 1 Niagara 尼加拉

   2 fall 瀑布

   3 favorite 最喜歡的

   4 waterfall 瀑布

2. The falls are big, beautiful and very loud.

   那裡的瀑布又大、又美,而且超大聲的。

   字彙輔助 1 big 大的

   2 beautiful 漂亮的

   3 very 非常

   4 loud 大聲的

3. And you get to travel to New York and Canada since it's right in the middle of the two places.

   而且你還可以順便去紐約或是加拿大旅行,因為它剛好在兩個地方的中間。

   字彙輔助 1 travel 旅行

   2 New York 紐約

3 Canada 加拿大

4 right 對的

5 middle 中間

4. At nighttime, the falls are even lighted up with color-ful lights.

在晚上的時候他們還會有各種顏色的燈亮起。

字彙輔助　1 nighttime 夜間

2 even 甚至

3 light up 點燃

4 colorful 多采多姿

5 light 燈

▶▶ 字彙、慣用語補充包

字彙、慣用語	中譯
One's face lights up	讓某人的眼睛為之一亮、讓某人開心
be drawn to	被吸引到……
Seven Natural Wonders	世界七大奇景
be always in awe of	對……感到震驚, 敬畏的
cannon ball	抱膝跳水

▶▶ 一氣呵成

Q1: What's your favorite waterfall? Why?

🎧 MP3 47

你最喜歡的瀑布是哪一個？為什麼呢？

Niagara Falls is my favorite waterfalls. The falls are big, beautiful and very loud. And you can get to travel to New York and Canada since it's right in the middle of the two places.

At nighttime the falls are even lighted up with colorful lights. I'm definitely going there for my honeymoon. It's just very romantic in general.

尼加拉瀑布是我最喜歡的瀑布。那裡的瀑布又大、又美，而且超大聲的。而且你還可以順便去紐約或是加拿大旅行，因為它剛好在兩個地方的中間。

在晚上的時候他們還會有不一樣顏色的燈亮起。我一定要去那裡度蜜月。整體來說那就是一個很浪漫的地方啊。

▶▶ 你來試試看

_____ is my favorite waterfalls. The falls
are _____. And you get to travel to____
_____
_____.

    At nighttime _____.
I'm definitely going there for my _____.
It's just very _____ in general.

    _____是我最喜歡的瀑布。那裡的瀑布_____
_____。而且你還可以順便去_____
_____。

    在晚上的時候_____。我一定要
去那裡_____。整體來說那就是一個很_____
____的地方阿。

UNIT 2 ▶▶ 瀑布

▶▶ 單句口說

1. There are so many things you can do at the waterfall.

   在瀑布有很多事情可以做。

   字彙輔助　① many 許多的
   　　　　　② things 事情
   　　　　　③ can 能夠
   　　　　　④ waterfall 瀑布

2. My friends and I like to jump off the rock and swim.

   我和我的朋友跟我都喜歡從石頭上跳下去游泳。

   字彙輔助　① friend 朋友
   　　　　　② jump off 跳下來
   　　　　　③ rock 岩石
   　　　　　④ swim 游泳

3. When the water is clean, it is the most refreshing feeling you get.

   當水很乾淨的時候，那是最令人覺得清新的感覺。

   字彙輔助　① when 當
   　　　　　② water 水

3 clean 乾淨

4 refreshing 令人覺得清新的

5 feeling 感覺

---

4. We usually do cannon ball or just dive under the waterfall.

我們通常都會抱膝跳水或是潛到瀑布底下。

字彙輔助 1 usually 通常

2 cannon ball 抱膝跳水

3 dive 潛水

4 under 在……之下

▶▶ 字彙、慣用語補充包

字彙、慣用語	中譯
take a step back	退後一步
result in	造成
natural remedy	天然療法
in the presence of	在……面前
Tell me about it!	我懂、我知道！

▶▶ 一氣呵成

Q2: What do you usually like to do at the water-falls? 🎧 MP3 48

你通常都喜歡在瀑布做什麼呢？

There are so many things you can do at the water-fall. My friends and I like to jump off the rock and swim. When the water is clean, it is the most refreshing feeling you get.

We usually do cannon ball or just dive under the waterfall. Of Course, we only jump off when it is safe at that place.

在瀑布有很多事情可以做。我和我的朋友都喜歡從石頭上跳下去游泳。當水很乾淨的時候，那是最令人覺得清新的感覺。

我們通常都會抱膝跳水或是潛到瀑布底下。當然，只有在安全的狀況之下我們才會跳水啦。

▶▶▶ 你來試試看

There are so many things you can do at the waterfall.
My friends and I like to _____.
When the water is clean, _____
_____.

We usually do_____.
Of Course,_____
_____.

在瀑布有很多事情可以做阿。我的朋友跟我都很喜歡____
_____。當水很乾淨的時候，_____
_____。

我們通常都會_____
_____。當然，_____
_____。

UNIT 3 ▶▶ 湖泊

▶▶ 單句口說

1. Campfire, fishing, and refreshing morning swims.

   營火、釣魚，還有清涼的晨泳。

   字彙輔助　❶ campfire 營火

   　　　　　❷ fishing 釣魚

   　　　　　❸ refreshing 令人感到清新的

   　　　　　❹ morning 早上

   　　　　　❺ swim 游泳

2. I think it would be so awesome to just stay a few days or weeks by the lake.

   我覺得如果可以在湖邊待上個幾天或是幾個禮拜一定會超棒的。

   字彙輔助　❶ awesome 很棒的

   　　　　　❷ stay 待在

   　　　　　❸ a few days 幾天

   　　　　　❹ weeks 幾週

   　　　　　❺ by the lake 在湖邊

3. I was in the Boy Scout growing up, and we would spend our summer by the lake and learn how to fish and camp.

我小時候有加入童子軍，暑假的時候我們會在湖邊學怎麼釣魚還有露營。

字彙輔助　 1 Boy Scout 童子軍

2 grow 成長

3 spend 花費

4 summer 夏天

5 camp 露營

4. The memory by the lake is definitely one of my favorite childhood memories.

我最喜歡的兒時回憶之一就是暑假在湖邊的時光。

字彙輔助　 1 memory 記憶

2 definitely 絕對是

3 favorite 最喜愛的

4 childhood 童年

▶▶ 字彙、慣用語補充包

字彙、慣用語	中譯
be into	很喜歡……
cost a fortune	非常貴、花了很多錢
see it myself	親眼看到
know how it is	你知道的、你懂的
long story short	長話短說

▶▶ 一氣呵成

Q3: What are your impressions of a lake?

🎧 MP3 49

你對湖的印象是什麼？

Campfire, fishing, and refreshing morning swims. I think it would be so awesome to just stay a few days or weeks by the lake. I was in the Boy Scout growing up, and we would spend our summer by the lake and learn how to fish and camp.

The memory by the lake is definitely one of my favorite childhood memories. The buddy I met there is still one of my best friends.

營火、釣魚，還有清涼的晨泳。我覺得如果可以在湖邊待上幾天或是幾個禮拜一定會超棒的。我小時候有加入童子軍，暑假的時候我們會在湖邊學怎麼釣魚還有露營。

我最喜歡的兒時回憶之一就是暑假在湖邊的時光。我在那邊認識的一個朋友現在還是我最好的朋友之一。

▶▶ 你來試試看

Campfire, fishing, and refreshing morning swims. I think it would be so awesome _____
_____ . I was in the Boy Scout growing up, and_____
_____
_____ .

The memory by the lake is definitely one of my favorite childhood memories. _____
_____ .

營火、釣魚，還有清涼的晨泳。我覺得如果可以在_____
_____一定會超棒
的。我小時候有加入童子軍，_____
_____ 。

我最喜歡的兒時回憶之一就是暑假在湖邊的時光。_____
_____
_____ 。

UNIT 4 ▶▶ 湖泊

▶▶ 單句口說

1. Lake Louise! I saw it on the magazine randomly, and I was very impressed with the hotel there.

露易絲湖！我有一次不小心在雜誌上看到就對那裡的飯店印象深刻。

字彙輔助　① Lake Louise 露易絲湖
　　　　　　② magazine 雜誌
　　　　　　③ randomly 隨意地
　　　　　　④ impressed 印象深刻
　　　　　　⑤ hotel 飯店

2. I heard it costs a fortune to stay there for a night, but I guess it's worth the money.

聽說在那住一晚超級貴，但我想應該是值得的。

字彙輔助　① heard 聽過
　　　　　　② fortune 財產、財富
　　　　　　③ stay 待在
　　　　　　④ guess 猜想
　　　　　　⑤ worth 值得

3. I tried to call the travel agency about one of their tour packages there, but it's all booked out.

我有試著打給旅行社問他們那裡其中一個行程，可是全部都
訂光了。

字彙輔助　1 try 試著
　　　　　2 travel 旅行
　　　　　3 travel agency 旅行社
　　　　　4 tour packages 旅遊行程
　　　　　5 booked out 訂光了

4. I've already made a reservation for the next summer though.

但我已經訂了明年暑假去那裡的行程。

字彙輔助　1 already 已經
　　　　　2 reservation 訂位
　　　　　3 next 下個
　　　　　4 summer 夏天
　　　　　5 though 雖然

▶▶ 字彙、慣用語補充包

字彙、慣用語	中譯
there is something about	……有某種令人無法解釋的元素
mind blowing	令人震撼的
heads up	提醒、提點
drama queen	戲劇化、小題大作的人
speaking from one's own experience	某人的經驗談

▶▶ 一氣呵成

Q4: Which lake do you want to visit? Why?

🎧 MP3 50

你最想要去哪一個湖？為什麼？

Lake Louise! I saw it on the magazine randomly, and I was very impressed with the hotel there. I heard it costs a fortune to stay there for a night, but I guess it's worth the money.

I tried to call the travel agency about one of their tour packages there, but it's all booked out. I've already made a reservation for the next summer though. It's one of the most fancy hotels, so I have to see it myself.

露易絲湖！我有一次不小心在雜誌上看到就對那裡的飯店印象深刻。聽說在那住一晚超級貴，但我想應該是值得的。

我有試著打給旅行社，問他們那裡的其中一個行程，可是全部都訂光了。但我已經訂了明年暑假去那裡的行程。那飯店是最豪華的飯店之一，我一定要親自瞧瞧。

▶▶ 你來試試看

_____ ! I saw it on the magazine randomly and I was very impressed with _____ there. I heard it __ _____ .

I tried to call the travel agency about one of their tour packages there, but _____ . I've already made a reservation for _____ _____ . It's one of the most fancy hotels, so _____ .

_____ ！我有一次不小心在雜誌上看到就對那裡的_____印象深刻。聽說在那_____ _____ 。

我有試著打給旅行社，問他們那裡的其中一個行程，可是 _____ 。但我已經訂了_____ _____ 。那飯店是最豪華的飯店之一，_____ 。

UNIT 5 ▶▶ 洞穴

▶▶ 單句口說

1. I randomly read about it on a magazine, while I was getting a haircut, and I have been really interested about going to see it.

我有次在剪頭髮的時候不經意在雜誌上看到的,然後我就一直想去看。

字彙輔助　❶ randomly 隨意地
　　　　　❷ read 閱讀
　　　　　❸ magazine 雜誌
　　　　　❹ haircut 剪頭髮
　　　　　❺ interest 興趣

2. It's said that the crystal formation in that cave is huge.

聽說在洞穴裡的水晶體十分巨大。

字彙輔助　❶ It's said that 據說……
　　　　　❷ crystal 水晶
　　　　　❸ formation 形成
　　　　　❹ cave 洞穴
　　　　　❺ huge 巨大的

3. It is over 9 meters long and 1 meter wide.

它有超過九公尺長，然後一公尺寬。

字彙輔助 　1 over 超過

　2 meter 公尺

　3 long 長

　4 wide 寬

4. I really want to see this giant crystal, but I heard it's disturbingly hot in that cave.

我真的很想去看這個巨型水晶，但是我聽說在洞穴裡是超級熱的。

字彙輔助 　1 really 真正地

　2 giant 巨大的

　3 hear 聽

　4 disturbingly 干擾地

▶▶ 字彙、慣用語補充包

字彙、慣用語	中譯
prepare for the worst	做最壞的打算
better safe than sorry	有備無患
come in handy	派上用途
comfort zone	舒適圈
stargazing	觀星

▶▶ 一氣呵成

Q5: What are some of the most interesting caves in the world? 🎧 MP3 51

世界上有哪一些有趣的洞穴呢？

Have you heard about the Cave of Crystals in Mexico? Doesn't it just sound so fascinating? I randomly read about it on a magazine, while I was getting a haircut, and I have been really interested about going to see it. It's said that the crystal formation in that cave is huge.

It is over 9 meters long and 1 meter wide. I really want to see this giant crystal, but I heard it's disturbingly hot in that cave. Well...no wonder the crystal is still there...

你有聽過墨西哥的巨型水晶洞穴嗎？你不覺得聽起來就很吸引人嗎？我有次在剪頭髮的時候不經意在雜誌上看到的，然後我就一直想去看。聽說在洞穴裡的水晶體十分巨大。

它有超過九公尺長，然後一公尺寬。我真的很想去看這個巨型水晶，但是我聽說在洞穴裡是超級熱的。哎……難怪那些水晶都還在那…

▶▶ 你來試試看

Have you heard about _____?
Doesn't it just sound so fascinating? I _____
_____, and I have been really interested about going
to see it. _____
_____.

_____.
I really want to see _____
_____. Well...no wonder
the crystal is still there...

你有聽過_____
__？你不覺得聽起來就很吸引人嗎？我_____
_____，然後我就一直想去看。
_____。

_____。
我真的很想去看_____
_____。 _____
_____。

口說『演練+實戰』

UNIT 6 ▶▶ 洞穴

▶▶ 單句口說

1. I've heard a lot of stories when people got stuck in the caves.

   我有聽過許多關於人們困在洞穴裡的許多故事。

   字彙輔助　1 hear 聽說

   2 a lot of 許多

   3 story 故事

   4 stuck 困住

   5 cave 洞穴

2. So, I think for me, I would want to bring extra food and water.

   所以我想對我來說，我會想要帶多點的食物和水。

   字彙輔助　1 think 認為

   2 want 想要

   3 bring 攜帶

   4 extra 額外的

   5 water 水

3. Ropes and warm clothes to prepare for the worst.

繩子和保暖的衣服用來做最壞的打算。

字彙輔助　1 rope 繩子

2 warm 溫暖的

3 clothes 衣物

4 prepare 準備

5 the worst 最糟的

4. I might sound paranoid, but better safe than sorry, right?

我聽起來好像有點神經質，可是有備無患，對吧？

字彙輔助　1 might 可能

2 sound 聽起來

3 paranoid 偏執狂的

4 safe 安全

5 sorry 遺憾

▶▶ 字彙、慣用語補充包

字彙、慣用語	中譯
ready or not	不管你準備好了沒有
glamping	豪華露營
high season	旺季
heaven on earth	人間天堂
cannot stress enough	強調非常重要

▶▶ 一氣呵成

Q6: What kind of equipment do you think you need to explore caves? 🎧 MP3 52

你覺得探索洞穴的時候需要哪一些配備呢？

I've heard a lot of stories when people got stuck in the caves. So, I think for me, I would want to bring extra food and water.

Ropes and warm clothes to prepare for the worst. I might sound paranoid, but better safe than sorry, right?

我有聽過許多關於人們困在洞穴裡的故事。所以我想對我來說，我會想要帶多點的食物和水。

繩子和保暖的衣服用來做最壞的打算。我聽起來好像有點神經質，可是有備無患，對吧？

⊪▶ 你來試試看

I've heard a lot of _____
_____. So, I think for me, _____
_____.

_____ to prepare for the worst. __
_____
_____.

　　我有聽過許多_____。
所以我想對我來說，_____
_____。

_____用來做最
壞的打算。_____
_____。

UNIT 7 ▶▶ 國家公園

▶▶ 單句口說

1. I've been to several National Parks in the world.

   我有去過全世界好幾個國家公園。

   字彙輔助 1 have been to 去過

   2 several 好幾個

   3 national 國家的

   4 park 公園

   5 world 世界

2. but I would tell you that Jiuzhaigou Vally National Park in China is just magical.

   但是我覺得最夢幻的是中國的九寨溝國家公園。

   字彙輔助 1 tell 告訴

   2 Jiuzhaigou 九寨溝

   3 National Park 國家公園

   4 China 中國

   5 magical 夢幻的

3. The five-colored lakes, the clear sky and the evergreen forests are just amazing on its own.

五色沼、晴朗的天空、常青的森林分開看就已經很美了。

字彙輔助　① five-colored 五色的

② lake 湖

③ clear 晴朗的

④ evergreen 常青的

⑤ amazing 驚人的

4. Heaven on earth would be the best description for it.

對它最好的描述就是人間天堂。

字彙輔助　① heaven 天堂

② earth 地球

③ best 最棒的

④ description 描述

▶▶ 字彙、慣用語補充包

字彙、慣用語	中譯
all that jazz	諸如此類的
off the record	私下說說
Déjà vu	似曾相似的
sweet deal	順心的交易、很棒的交易
up to whatever	什麼都可以

⏩ 一氣呵成

Q7: **Have you ever been to any National Parks? If not, which one do you want to visit?** 🎧 MP3 53

你有去過國家公園嗎？沒有的話，你想要去哪一個國家公園呢？

I've been to several National Parks in the world, but I would tell you that Jiuzhaigou Vally National Park in China is just magical.

The five-colored lakes, the clear sky and the ever-green forests are just amazing on its own. Heaven on earth would be the best description for it.

我有去過全世界好幾個國家公園，但是我覺得最夢幻的是中國的九寨溝國家公園。五色沼、晴朗的天空、常青的森林分開看就已經很美了。對它最好的描述就是人間天堂。

▶▶ 你來試試看

I've been to several National Parks in the world, but ____

_____

_____

_____ .

_____

_____

_____ . _____

_____ would be the best description for it.

我有去過全世界好幾個國家公園，但是_____

_____ 。

_____

_____ 。對它最好的描述就是_____

_____ 。

UNIT 8 ▶▶ 國家公園

▶▶ 單句口說

1. I expect to see a lot of wildlife in the National Parks for sure.

   我當然是期待在國家公園裡看到很多野生動物。

   字彙輔助　1 expect 期待
   2 see 看到
   3 a lot of 許多
   4 wildlife 野生動物
   5 for sure 確定、當然

2. Some National Parks even give out maps of where to see those animals.

   有些國家公園甚至會給你地圖去看那些動物。

   字彙輔助　1 some 有些
   2 even 甚至
   3 give out 給
   4 map 地圖
   5 animal 動物

3. Bear, bighorn, sheep, bison, elk, and river otters all wander in the parks.

熊、大角羊、綿羊、美洲野牛、麋鹿和水獺都在公園裡到處遊蕩。

字彙輔助　① bighorn 大角羊
　　　　　　　② sheep 綿羊
　　　　　　　③ bison 美洲野牛
　　　　　　　④ elk 麋鹿
　　　　　　　⑤ river otter 水獺
　　　　　　　⑥ wander 遊蕩

4. It was frightening, but also amazing to see a bear in such a short distance.

其實蠻恐怖的，但是同時也是很神奇的是可以這麼近看著熊。

字彙輔助　① frightening 恐怖的
　　　　　　　② amazing 驚人的
　　　　　　　③ see 看到
　　　　　　　④ bear 熊
　　　　　　　⑤ distance 距離

▶▶ 字彙、慣用語補充包

字彙、慣用語	中譯
add the characters	為……增添特色
period	句點、就是這樣
blah-blah-blah	無聊的話、廢話
it's only natural	很自然的
getting out of hand	失去控制

▶▶ 一氣呵成

Q2: What are the things you expect to see or do in the National Parks? 🎧 MP3 54
你期待在國家公園裡看到或做什麼?

I expect to see a lot of wildlife in the National Parks for sure. Some National Parks even give out maps of where to see those animals. Bear, bighorn sheep, bison, elk, and river otters all wander in the parks. I was once really close to a bear.

It was frightening, but also amazing to see a bear in such a short distance. I was in awe to see such a beautiful creature in the National Park and I would love to see more of them.

我當然是期待在國家公園裡看到很多野生動物。有些國家公園甚至會給你地圖去看那些動物。熊、大角羊、美洲野牛、麋鹿和水獺都在公園裡到處遊蕩。我有一次很接近一隻熊。

其實蠻恐怖的,但是同時也是很神奇的是可以這麼近看著熊。我那時候看到這麼美的生物真的很震撼,我還想要再看多一些。

▶▶ 你來試試看

I expect to see a lot of _____ in the National Parks for sure. Some National Parks even give out maps of where to see those animals.

_____

_____

_____.

    It was frightening, but a _____.
I was in awe to see such a beautiful creature in the National Parks and _____

_____.

我當然是期待在國家公園裡看到_____
_____。有些國家公園甚至會給你地圖去看那些動物。

_____

_____

_____。

其實蠻恐怖的，但是_____
_____。我那時候看到這麼美的生物真的很震撼，
_____。

UNIT 9 ▶▶ 大峽谷

▶▶ 單句口說

1. I was traveling in Tibet, and had a chance to visit the Yurlung Tsangpo Canyon.

   我有去西藏旅行然後有機會拜訪雅魯藏波峽谷。

   字彙輔助　1 travel 旅行
   　　　　　　　2 Tibet 西藏
   　　　　　　　3 chance 機會
   　　　　　　　4 visit 參觀
   　　　　　　　5 Yurlung Tsangpo 雅魯藏波
   　　　　　　　6 canyon 峽谷

2. They claimed that it was the highest river in the world, and that's why the name of the canyon meant "The Everest of Rivers".

   他們號稱那裡是世界上最高的河流，那也是峽谷以此命名的原因。意思是說那是河流裡的聖母峰。

   字彙輔助　1 claim 宣稱
   　　　　　　　2 highest 最高的
   　　　　　　　3 river 溪流
   　　　　　　　4 The Everest of Rivers 聖母峰

3. It is a place that's really close to heaven I think.

而且我也覺得那裡是最接近天堂的地方。

字彙輔助　1 place 地方

　　　　　2 really 真正地

　　　　　3 close 接近

　　　　　4 heaven 天堂

　　　　　5 think 認為

4. Very pure and clean.

非常的純淨跟乾淨。

字彙輔助　1 very 非常

　　　　　2 pure 純淨

　　　　　3 clean 乾淨

▶▶ 字彙、慣用語補充包

字彙、慣用語	中譯
kick back	放輕鬆
pitch dark	漆黑的
well-deserved	非常應得的、當之無愧的
drag	累贅
bundle up	包起來、穿得很保暖
live up to my dad's expectation	達到我父親的期望

▶▶ 一氣呵成

Q9: Have you ever been to any canyon? 🎧 **MP3 55**
　　你有曾經去過任何峽谷嗎？

　　I was traveling in Tibet, and had a chance to visit the Yurlung Tsangpo Canyon. They claimed that it was the highest river in the world, and that's why the name of the canyon meant "The Everest of Rivers". It is a place that's really close to heaven I think. Very pure and clean.

　　我有去西藏旅行然後有機會拜訪雅魯藏波峽谷。他們號稱那裡是世界上最高的河流，那也是峽谷以此命名的原因。意思是説那是河流裡的聖母峰。而且我也覺得那裡是最接近天堂的地方。非常的純淨跟乾淨。

▶▶▶ 你來試試看

I was traveling in _____ , and had a chance to visit _____
_____ . They claimed that it
was _____ ,
and_____ . _____
_____ . _____
_____ .

　　我有去_____玩然後去了_____ 。
他們號稱那裡是_____ 。
_____ 。 _____
_____ 。 _____ 。

UNIT 10 ▶▶ 大峽谷

▶▶ 單句口說

1. Well...it's mostly because we heard these places during the geography class when we were growing up.

   嗯...我想大多是因為我們以前在上地理課的時候就有聽過這些地方。

   字彙輔助　**1** mostly 主要地
   　　　　　　2 hear 聽到
   　　　　　　3 place 地方
   　　　　　　4 geography 地理
   　　　　　　5 grow 生長

2. You know the name, and then you started watching Discovery or National Geographic Channel.

   你就知道那些名字，然後你就開始看探索頻道或是國家地理頻道。

   字彙輔助　**1** know 知道
   　　　　　　2 start 開始
   　　　　　　3 watch 觀看
   　　　　　　4 Discovery 探索頻道
   　　　　　　5 National Geographical Channel 國家地理頻道

3. It's one of the most amazing things, and it must be true because the textbooks and Discovery and National Geographic don't lie.

那是世界上最令人感到驚奇的事物之一，而且也一定是真實的，因為課本、探索頻道還有國家地理頻道不會騙人。

字彙輔助　❶ amazing 驚人的

　　　　　❷ true 真的

　　　　　❸ textbooks 教科書

4. The next thing you know, you're posting a picture on Facebook of you and the canyon.

接下來你就發現你正在臉書上發佈一張你跟峽谷的照片。

字彙輔助　❶ next 下個

　　　　　❷ know 知道

　　　　　❸ post 發佈……消息

　　　　　❹ picture 圖片

　　　　　❺ canyon 峽谷

▶▶ 字彙、慣用語補充包

字彙、慣用語	中譯
that's a tough one	那個蠻難的
quality time	親密時光
grow on	感染、影響
touch base with	和……聯繫
my kind of	我喜歡的那種……

▶▶ 一氣呵成

Q10: Why do you think canyons are so popular?

🎧 MP3 56

你覺得為什麼峽谷很受歡迎呢？

Well...it's mostly because we heard these places during the geography class when we were growing up. You know the name, and then you started watching Discovery or National Geographic channel.

It's one of the most amazing things, and it must be true because the textbooks and Discovery and National Geographic don't lie. The next thing you know, you're posting a picture on Facebook of you and the canyon.

嗯……我想大多是因為我們以前在上地理課的時候就有聽過這些地方，你就知道那些名字。然後你就開始看探索頻道或是國家地理頻道。

那是世界上最令人感到驚人的事物之一，而且也一定是真實的，因為課本、探索頻道還有國家地理頻道不會騙人。接下來你就發現你正在臉書上發佈一張你跟峽谷的照片。

▶▶ 你來試試看

Well...it's mostly because _____

_____ You know the name, and _____

_____ .

It's one of the most amazing things, and _____

_____

_____ . The next thing you know, you_____

_____ .

嗯⋯⋯我想大多是因為_____

_____，你就知道那些名字。_____

_____。

那是世界上最驚人的事物之一，而且_____

_____。然後你就發現你_____

_____。

UNIT 11 ▶▶ Sunrise 日出

▶▶ 單句口說

1. There is something magical and holy about it.

   我覺得它有一種很神奇跟神聖的感覺。

   字彙輔助　① There is 有
   ② something 某事
   ③ magical 魔術的
   ④ holy 神聖的

2. Many people go all the way to the mountain just to bid their good morning to the sun.

   許多人爬上去就只是為了要跟太陽說早安。

   字彙輔助　① many 許多
   ② mountain 山
   ③ bid 向……表示
   ④ good 好的、令人滿意的
   ⑤ morning 早晨

3. It's really something to see up there.

   上去之後看到的美景真的蠻棒的。

   字彙輔助　① really 真正的
   ② something 重要的人或事物
   ③ see 看到

4. However, in exchange, you have to wake up so early that you might as well just stay up late.

然而，要看到這美景，你就得要很早起床。早到你乾脆熬夜不要睡好了。

字彙輔助　**1** however 然而

　　　　　　2 in exchange 相對而言

　　　　　　3 have to 必須

　　　　　　4 wake up 起床

　　　　　　5 stay up late 熬夜

▶▶ 字彙、慣用語補充包

字彙、慣用語	中譯
eat her alive	生吞
spork	匙叉
have a blast	玩得很開心
make a big fuss	小題大作
prove them wrong	向……證明他是錯的

▶▶ 一氣呵成

Q11: Do you like watching sunrise? Why or why not? 🎧 MP3 57

你喜歡看日出嗎？為什麼或為什麼不？

I do really like sunrise. There is something magical and holy about it. Many people go all the way to the mountain just to bid their good morning to the sun. It's really something to see up there.

However, in exchange, you have to wake up so early that you might as well just stay up late. I drank so much coffee that I was shaking.

我真的很喜歡日出。我覺得它有一種很神奇跟神聖的感覺。許多人爬上去就只是為了要跟太陽說早安。上去之後看到的美景真的蠻棒的。

但是，要看到這美景，你就得很早起床。早到你乾脆熬夜不要睡好了。我那時候喝超多咖啡，喝到我都抖了起來。

▶▶ 你來試試看

I do really like sunrise. There is something _____
_____. Many people go all the way to the
mountain just to _____
_____. It's really something to see up there.

However, in exchange, _____. _____
_____.

我真的很喜歡日出。我覺得它有一種_____
_____。很多人爬上去就只是為了要_____
_____。上去之後看到的美景真
的蠻棒的。

但是，要看到這美景，_____
_____。 _____。
_____。

UNIT 12 ▶▶ Sunrise 日出

▶▶ 單句口說

1. When I was there, I had to lower myself to everyone's level to get in the tiny train for getting up to the mountain.

   想當初我去看的時候，可是勉強和大家一起搭乘小火車上山去的。

   字彙輔助　1 lower myself 降格
   2 everyone 每個人
   3 level 等級
   4 tiny 微小的
   5 mountain 山脈

2. I'd always imagined that we'd get in a luxurious chariot at 3 or 4 in the morning and just wave around the sparklers.

   我一直覺得該乘坐豪華馬車，在凌晨三四點左右，邊乘著馬車邊拿著仙女棒朝著天空劃呀劃的。

   字彙輔助　1 imagine 想像
   2 luxurious 奢華的
   3 chariot 馬車
   4 wave 揮舞
   5 sparkler 仙女棒

3. So dreamy, and then some servers would have the delicious food ready on the side when you were enjoying the sunrise.

蠻夢幻的。然後隨從們還準備了美食在旁，在看日出時能享用。

字彙輔助　1 dreamy 夢幻的
　　　　　2 server 隨從
　　　　　3 delicious 好吃的
　　　　　4 enjoy 享受
　　　　　5 sunrise 日出

4. I guess they didn't live up to my expectation at all!

我想他們一點也沒有我預期的那麼好。

字彙輔助　1 guess 猜想
　　　　　2 live up to... 達到……標準
　　　　　3 expectation 期待
　　　　　4 not... at all 一點也不

▶▶ 字彙、慣用語補充包

字彙、慣用語	中譯
altitude sickness	高山症
I don't do	我不……
take my mind off	轉移你從……上的注意力、不要一直想……
pros and cons	優勢和劣勢
X will always be X	……永遠就是這樣

▶▶ 一氣呵成

Q12: Where have you seen the most beautiful sunrise? 🎧 MP3 58

你在哪裡看過最美的日出？

Sunrise? Of course at Mountain Ali in Taiwan! Where else do you go? When I was there, I had to lower myself to everyone's level to get in the tiny train for getting up to the mountain.

I'd always imagined that we'd get in a luxurious chariot at 3 or 4 in the morning and just wave around the sparklers. So dreamy, and then some servers would have the delicious food ready on the side when you were enjoying the sunrise. I guess they didn't live up to my expectation at all!

　　看日出？當然是要去阿里山啊？不然你覺得還有什麼地方好去？想當初我去看的時候，可是勉強和大家一起搭乘小火車上山去的？

　　我一直覺得該乘坐豪華馬車，在凌晨三四點左右，邊乘著馬車邊拿著仙女棒朝著天空劃呀劃的。蠻夢幻的。然後隨從們還準備了好美食在旁，在看日出時能享用。我想他們一點也沒有我預期的那麼好。

▶▶ 你來試試看

Sunrise? Of course at _____!
Where else do you go? When I was there, _____
_____
_____.

I'd always imagined that _____
_____.
_____. I
guess they didn't live up to my expectation at all!

　　看日出？當然是要去_____？不然你覺得還有什
麼地方好去？_____？

　　我一直覺得該_____
_____。_____
_____。我想他們一點也沒有我預期的那麼
好。

UNIT 13 ▶▶ Camping 露營

▶▶ 單句口說

1. A water bottle and iodine are always good to have when you need to track down the water source.

   如果你需要找水源的話，有水壺和碘在身邊的話是很好的。

   字彙輔助　❶ a water bottle 水壺
   　　　　　❷ iodine 碘
   　　　　　❸ always 總是
   　　　　　❹ track down 追溯
   　　　　　❺ water source 水源

2. I bring my fishing pole with me whenever I'm going to be close to the water.

   如果會在水邊露營的話，我也都會帶我的釣魚竿。

   字彙輔助　❶ bring 攜帶
   　　　　　❷ fishing pole 釣魚竿
   　　　　　❸ whenever 每當
   　　　　　❹ close 接近
   　　　　　❺ water 水

3. It's good to kill time, and you might catch a nutritional dinner.

那是很好打發時間的方式，而且說不定你有可能會抓到你的營養晚餐。

字彙輔助　1 good 好的
2 kill time 打發時間
3 might 可能
4 catch 抓住
5 nutritional 營養的

4. Most importantly, an open mind is always good since you never know who you are going to run into.

最重要的是，心胸開闊總是好的，因為你永遠不知道你會遇到誰。

字彙輔助　1 most importantly 最重要的是
2 open 開放的
3 since 因為
4 know 知道
5 run into 遇見

▶▶ 字彙、慣用語補充包

字彙、慣用語	中譯
don't get me wrong	不要誤會我
work it off	消耗掉……
knock on your door	……來敲門
sustainable	永續發展的
You never know	很難說

▶▶ 一氣呵成

Q13: What are some of the most important things to bring when you go camping? 🎧 MP3 59
哪些重要的東西是你露營的時候會帶的？

A water bottle and iodine are always good to have when you need to track down the water source. I bring my fishing pole with me whenever I'm going to be close to the water. It's good to kill time, and you might catch a nutritional dinner. You never know!

Most importantly, an open mind is always good since you never know who you are going to run into. I love to talk to people and listen to their stories. An open mind usually leads me to the most amazing experiences.

如果你需要找水源的話，有水壺和碘在身邊的話是很好的。我也都會帶我的釣魚竿如果我知道我會在水邊露營的話。那是很好打發時間的方式，而且說不定你有可能會抓到你的營養晚餐。

最重要的是，心胸開闊總是好的，因為你永遠不知道你會遇到誰。我很喜歡跟別人聊天和聽他們的故事。心胸開闊總是帶給我很美好的經驗。

▶▶ 你來試試看

_____ is always good to have when you need to track down the water source. I bring my fishing pole with me whenever I'm going to be close to the water. _____
_____. _____!

　　Most importantly, _____.
I love to talk to people and listen to their stories. _____
_____.

_____，有水壺和碘在身邊的話是很好的。我也都會帶我的釣魚竿如果會在水邊露營的話，我也都會帶我的釣魚竿。_____
_____。

　　最重要的是，_____
_____。我很喜歡跟別人聊天和聽他們的故事。__
_____
_____。

UNIT 14 ▶▶ Camping 露營

▶▶ 單句口說

1. I had a blast when I was at Jasper National Park last year.

   我去年在賈斯柏國家公園裡玩得很開心。

   字彙輔助 ❶ had a blast 玩得開心

   ❷ when 當

   ❸ Jasper 賈斯柏

   ❹ National Park 國家公園

   ❺ last year 去年

2. There are countless beautiful lakes where you can go kayaking, fishing, white water rafting, etc.

   那裡有數不清的美麗湖泊，在那裡你可以划塑膠皮艇、釣魚和泛舟等等。

   字彙輔助 ❶ countless 數不清的

   ❷ beautiful 漂亮的

   ❸ kayaking 划塑膠皮艇

   ❹ fishing 釣魚

   ❺ water rafting 泛舟

3. I met some really cool world travelers at the campsite that evening.

我那天晚上在營地也遇到一些實在有夠酷的世界旅行家。

字彙輔助　**1** meet 遇見

　　　　　2 really 真正地

　　　　　3 world 世界

　　　　　4 campsite 營地

　　　　　5 evening 晚上

4. We spent our evening playing music and share stories under the stars.

我們那天晚上就在星空下玩音樂和分享彼此的故事中度過。

字彙輔助　**1** spend 花費

　　　　　2 play 玩

　　　　　3 music 音樂

　　　　　4 share 分享

　　　　　5 story 故事

▶▶ 字彙、慣用語補充包

字彙、慣用語	中譯
It just might be your lucky day	今天可能換你……
let alone	更別提
I'm tired of	我受夠……
you beat me on this one	你考倒我了！
I don't have a clue	我不知道、我一點線索也沒有

▶▶ 一氣呵成

Q14: What is your best camping experience?

🎧 MP3 60

你最棒的露營經驗是什麼呢？

I had a blast when I was at Jasper National Park last year. There are countless beautiful lakes where you can go kayaking, fishing, white water rafting, etc. You name it.

I met some really cool world travelers at the campsite that evening. We spent our evening playing music and sharing stories under the stars.

我去年在賈斯柏國家公園裡玩得很開心。那裡有數不清的美麗湖泊，在那裡你可以划塑膠皮艇，釣魚，和泛舟等等。你説得出來的都有。

我那天晚上在營地也遇到一些實在有夠酷的世界旅行家。我們那天晚上就在星空下玩音樂和分享彼此的故事中度過。

▶▶ 你來試試看

I had a blast when I was at _____
last year. _____
_____. You name it.

I met some really cool world travelers at the campsite
that evening. _____
_____.

我去年在_____裡玩得
很開心。_____

_____

_____。你說得出來的都有。

我那天晚上在營地也遇到一些實在有夠酷的世界旅行家。

_____

_____。

255

UNIT 15 ▶▶ 爬山健行

▶▶ 單句口說

1. I like to stop frequently to enjoy the scenery, the view, and the flora and the fauna.

   我很喜歡一直停下來享受周遭的風景、景色、還有花草跟動物。

   字彙輔助　1 stop 停止

   　　　　　2 frequently 頻繁地

   　　　　　3 enjoy 享受

   　　　　　4 scenery 風景

   　　　　　5 view 景色

   　　　　　6 flora 植物

   　　　　　7 fauna 動物

2. so it's best when the hike has a great view for me to stop and take pictures.

   所以如果是一個可以一直讓我停下來拍照的漂亮步道最好。

   字彙輔助　1 best 最棒的

   　　　　　2 hike 健行

   　　　　　3 great 很棒的

   　　　　　4 view 景色

   　　　　　5 take pictures 照相

3. preferably a shaded hike.

更好地是還有遮蔭的步道。

字彙輔助　1 preferably 更好地

2 shaded 遮蔭的

3 hike 步道

4. just so that it's more comfortable walking long distances.

所以長途走下來也比較舒服。

字彙輔助　1 so 所以

2 more 更

3 comfortable 舒適的

4 walking 行走

5 distance 距離

▶▶ 字彙、慣用語補充包

字彙、慣用語	中譯
namaste	我祝福你、謝謝（瑜珈用語）
blend in	混熟
What a steal!	超划算的！超便宜的！
It makes so much sense	⋯⋯超說得通的
That's something for me!	對我來說很了不起！

▶▶ 一氣呵成

Q15: What kind of hikes do you enjoy? 🎧 MP3 61
你喜歡怎麼樣的健行呢？

I like to stop frequently to enjoy the scenery, the view, and the flora and the fauna, so it's best when the hike has a great view for me to stop and take pictures; preferably a shaded hike, just so that it's more comfortable walking long distances.

我很喜歡一直停下來享受周遭的風景、景色、還有花草跟動物，所以如果是一個可以一直讓我停下來拍照的漂亮步道最好。更好地是還有遮蔭的步道，所以長途走下來也比較舒服。

▶▶ 你來試試看

I like to stop frequently to enjoy the scenery, the view, and the flora and the fauna, so _____
_____
_____
_____.

　　我很喜歡一直停下來享受周遭的風景、景色、還有花草跟動物，所以_____
_____。_____
_____
_____。

UNIT 16 ▶▶ 爬山健行

▶▶ 單句口說

1. The best hike I've ever done is the trek to Everest Base Camp in Nepal.

   我去過最棒的是尼泊爾的聖母峰基地營健行。

   字彙輔助　**1** best 最棒的
   　　　　　2 hike 健行
   　　　　　3 trek 艱苦跋涉
   　　　　　4 Everest Base Camp 聖母峰基地營
   　　　　　5 Nepal 尼泊爾

2. The scenery can't be beat, and you get to take a look at Mt. Everest or Chomolungma, which means the "Goddess Mother of the World."

   風景無可匹敵，而且你還可以看到聖母峰，或是 Chomolungma（聖母峰藏文），也就是「世界之母」的意思。

   字彙輔助　**1** scenery 風景
   　　　　　2 beat 擊敗
   　　　　　3 take a look 看
   　　　　　4 Mt. Everest 聖母峰
   　　　　　5 Goddess Mother of the World 世界之母

3. It's spectacular just to see the highest point on planet Earth.

可以從世界最高點看下去真的是很壯觀。

字彙輔助　**1** spectacular 壯觀的

　　　　　2 just 只是

　　　　　3 highest 最高的

　　　　　4 point 點

　　　　　5 planet 行星

　　　　　6 Earth 地球

4. In May, the rhododendrons are in bloom with orchids growing in them.

在五月的時候，杜鵑花會和蘭花一起盛開。

字彙輔助　**1** May 五月

　　　　　2 rhododendron 杜鵑花

　　　　　3 in bloom 盛開

　　　　　4 orchid 蘭花

　　　　　5 grow 成長

▶▶ 字彙、慣用語補充包

字彙、慣用語	中譯
positive vibes	正面能量
pop up in my mind	想到
That said	……也就是說
universal language	世界共通的語言
under the impression	以為、覺得

▶▶ 一氣呵成

Q16: What is the best hike you have ever done? How was it? 🎧 MP3 62

你健行過最好的步道是哪裡？那個步道怎麼樣呢？

The best hike I've ever done is the trek to Everest Base Camp in Nepal. The people are incredible. The scenery can't be beat, and you get to take a look at Mt. Everest or Chomolungma, which means the "Goddess Mother of the World." It's spectacular just to see the highest point on planet Earth.

In May, the rhododendrons are in bloom with orchids growing in them. There are guesthouses on the way up. You can get a beer. Who knows, I might wander up there again.

　　我去過最棒的是尼泊爾的聖母峰基地營健行。那裡的人都好得不可思議，風景無可匹敵，而且你還可以看到聖母峰，或是 Chomolungma（聖母峰藏文），也就是「世界之母」的意思。可以從世界最高點看下去真的是很壯觀。

　　在五月的時候，杜鵑花會和蘭花一起盛開。在上去的路上也會遇到民宿，而你也可以在那買瓶啤酒。誰知道，我可能會再遊蕩上去一次。

▶▶ 你來試試看

The best hike I've ever done is the trek to _____
_____. The people
are incredible. The scenery can't be beat, and you get to
take a look at _____
_____. _____
_____
_____.

In May, _____
_____. There are guesthouses on the way up. _____
_____. Who knows, I might wander up there
again.

　　我去過最棒的是_____
_____。那裡的人都好得不可思議，風景無可匹敵，而
且你還可以看到_____
_____
_____ 。

　　在五月的時候，_____ 。
在上去的路上也會遇到民宿_____
_____。誰知道，我可能會再遊蕩上去一次。

UNIT 17 ▶▶ 釣魚

▶▶ **單句口說**

1. I kept thinking whoever came up with fishing was such a genius.

   我一直在想當初第一個發明釣魚這件事的人真是個天才。

   字彙輔助 1 keep 繼續

   2 think 想

   3 whoever 無論是誰

   4 come up with 想出

   5 genius 天才

   ....

2. He must have been so thrilled when he found out it actually worked!

   他那時候發現真的釣得到魚時一定超興奮的！

   字彙輔助 1 thrilled 興奮的

   3 find out 發現

   3 actually 真正地

   4 work 起作用、行得通

   ....

3. It's actually a lot more complicated than what it looks like.

其實釣魚比看起來還要複雜很多。

字彙輔助　**1** a lot 很多

　　　　　2 more 更

　　　　　3 complicated 複雜的

　　　　　4 look like 看起來

4. How to tie the knots, hook on the baits, fight the fish, even how to reel the fish in.

你要知道怎麼綁魚線的結，怎麼樣把魚餌勾在鉤上，怎麼和魚搏鬥，怎麼把魚拉進來。

字彙輔助　**1** tie 綁

　　　　　2 knot 結

　　　　　3 hook 鉤住

　　　　　4 bait 魚餌

　　　　　5 reel 拉

▶▶ 字彙、慣用語補充包

字彙、慣用語	中譯
I got you covered	有我在！
turn my world upside down	讓我的世界神魂顛倒、讓我的世界翻天覆地的
there's still a fine line between	在……之間還是有一線之隔
chicken out	退縮
get into......	進入……的領域

▶▶ 一氣呵成

Q17: Are you interested in fishing? Why? Why not? 🎧 MP3 63

你對釣魚有興趣嗎？為什麼有或為什麼沒有？

I'm very interested in fishing. It's so exciting when you have a fish on. I kept thinking whoever came up with fishing was such a genius. He must have been so thrilled when he found out it actually worked!

It's actually a lot more complicated than what it looks like. How to tie the knots, hook on the baits, fight the fish, even how to reel the fish in. It just feels really good, when you do everything right and catch a fish yourself.

我對釣魚超有興趣的。魚上鉤的時候真的是超刺激的。我一直在想當初第一個發明釣魚這件事的人真是個天才。他那時候發現真的釣得到魚時一定超興奮的！

其實釣魚比看起來還要複雜很多。你要知道怎麼綁魚線的結，怎麼樣把魚餌勾在鉤上，怎麼和魚搏鬥，怎麼把魚拉進來。當你把每一件事都做好然後再抓到魚的時候真的感覺超棒的！

▶▶ 你來試試看

I'm very interested in fishing. _____
_____. I kept thinking _____
_____. _____
_____!

It's actually a lot more complicated than what it looks
like. _____.
It just feels really good, when you do everything right and
catch a fish yourself.

我對釣魚超有興趣的。_____
_____。我都一直在想_____
_____。 _____
_____！

其實釣魚比看起來還要複雜很多。_____
_____。當你把每一件事都做好然後再抓到魚的時
候真的感覺超棒的！

UNIT 18 ▶▶ Fishing 釣魚

▶▶ **單句口說**

1. I've tried a lot of different kinds of fishing.

   我有試過很多種不同的釣魚方式。

   字彙輔助　❶ try 試過
   　　　　　❷ a lot of 很多
   　　　　　❸ different 不同的
   　　　　　❹ kinds of 種類
   　　　　　❺ fishing 釣魚

2. Deep-sea fishing, fresh water fishing, kayak fishing, Jet ski fishing, spear fishing...etc.

   深海釣魚、淡水釣魚、皮艇釣魚、水上摩托車釣魚和魚叉獵魚等等。

   字彙輔助　❶ deep-sea fishing 深海釣魚
   　　　　　❷ fresh water fishing 淡水釣魚
   　　　　　❸ kayak fishing 皮艇釣魚
   　　　　　❹ Jet ski fishing 水上摩托車釣魚
   　　　　　❺ spear fishing 魚叉獵魚

3. I have to say that I like kayak fishing the best because kayaking is a good exercise and it's just you and your

fishing poles out there.

不過我必須要說我最喜歡皮艇釣魚，因為它是很好的運動，而且你只需要你和你的釣竿。

字彙輔助　① have to 必須
　　　　　② like 喜歡
　　　　　③ best 最棒的
　　　　　④ exercise 運動
　　　　　⑤ fishing pole 釣竿

4. Really nice. I think everyone should try at least once.

真的很棒。我覺得每個人至少都要嘗試一次。

字彙輔助　① really 真的
　　　　　② nice 好的
　　　　　③ everyone 每個人
　　　　　④ try 試試看
　　　　　⑤ at least 至少

▶▶ 字彙、慣用語補充包

字彙、慣用語	中譯
the leap of faith	義無反顧的行動
cross my heart	我保證
see you on the flip side	待會見、改天見
live in the moment	活在當下
When it comes to	說到…

▶▶ 一氣呵成

Q18: What kind of fishing have you tried? How was it? 🎧 MP3 64

你試過怎麼樣的釣魚方式？好玩嗎？

I've tried a lot of different kinds of fishing. Deep-sea fishing, fresh water fishing, kayak fishing, Jet ski fishing, spear fishing...etc. You name it.

I have to say that I like kayak fishing the best because kayaking is a good exercise and it's just you and your fishing poles out there. Really nice. I think everyone should try at least once.

我有試過很多種不同的釣魚方式。深海釣魚、淡水釣魚、皮艇釣魚、水上摩托車釣魚和魚叉獵魚等等。你說得出來的幾乎都有。

不過我必須要說我最喜歡皮艇釣魚，因為它是很好的運動，而且你只需要你和你的釣竿。真的很棒。我覺得每個人至少都要嘗試一次。

▶▶ **你來試試看**

I've tried a lot of different kinds of fishing. _____

_____

_____

_____ .

I have to say that I like_____

_____

_____

_____

_____ .

我有試過很多種不同的釣魚方式。_____

_____

_____

_____ 。

不過我必須要說我最喜歡_____

_____

_____

_____ 。

UNIT 19 ▶▶ 瑜珈

▶▶ 單句口說

1. I think the time when I went to the Wanderlust Festival in Melbourne was a pretty memorable one.

   我覺得我在墨爾本的時候參加的 Wanderlust 節還蠻令人印象深刻的。

   字彙輔助　
   1 think 想
   2 festival 節慶
   3 Melbourne 墨爾本
   4 pretty 非常
   5 memorable 值得回憶的

2. It was a huge event and there were so many people doing yoga and meditation with you.

   那是一個超大的活動,而且也有很多人在那跟你一起做瑜珈和靜坐。

   字彙輔助　
   1 huge 巨大的
   2 event 活動
   3 many 許多
   4 yoga 瑜珈
   5 meditation 沉思

3. Everyone that joined the event was all really cool and with really positive vibes.

每位參加的人都很酷而且也有很多正面的能量。

字彙輔助　**1** everyone 每個人

　　　　　　2 join 參加

　　　　　　3 event 活動

　　　　　　4 cool 酷的

　　　　　　5 positive 正面的

　　　　　　6 vibe 能量

4. It was definitely something different. I really had a great time.

真的很不一樣，我真的玩得很開心。

字彙輔助　**1** definitely 明確地、肯定地

　　　　　　2 something 某事

　　　　　　3 different 不同的

　　　　　　4 really 真的

　　　　　　5 have a great time 玩得很開心

▶▶ 字彙、慣用語補充包

字彙、慣用語	詞性	中譯
end up		結果⋯⋯、到頭來⋯⋯
a blessing in disguise		因禍得福
It was a close call		真是危急、真的好險
I has butterflies in my stomach		因為緊張而坐立難安
takes me down memory lane		帶你回憶

▶▶ 一氣呵成

Q19: What is your best yoga experience? 🎧 MP3 65
你最棒的瑜伽體驗是什麼？

I think the time when I went to the Wanderlust Festival in Melbourne was a pretty memorable one. It was a huge event and there were so many people doing yoga and meditation with you.

Everyone that joined the event was all really cool and with really positive vibes. It was definitely something different. I really had a great time.

　　我覺得我在墨爾本的時候參加的 Wanderlust 節還蠻令人印象深刻的。那是一個超大的活動，而且也有很多人在那跟你一起做瑜珈和靜坐。每位參加的人都很酷而且也有很多正面的能量。真的很不一樣。我真的玩得很開心。

▶▶ 你來試試看

I think the time when I went to _____

_____ was a pretty memorable

one. It was a huge event and _____

_____.

Everyone that joined the event was all really cool and with really positive vibes. It was definitely something different. I really had a great time.

我覺得我在_____

__還蠻令人印象深刻的。那是一個超大的活動而且_____

_____。

參加的人都很酷而且也有很多正面的能量。真的很不一樣。我真的玩得很開心。

UNIT 20 ▸▸ Yoga 瑜珈

▸▸ **單句口說**

1. Oh, I personally don't remember one, but I can tell you a story from a friend of mine.

   喔，我本身是一個都不記得啦，但我可以跟你說我一個朋友的故事。

   字彙輔助　1 personally 個人地
   　　　　　2 remember 記住
   　　　　　3 tell 告訴
   　　　　　4 story 故事
   　　　　　5 friend 朋友

2. So she said she was wearing these really cool and brand-named workout leggings.

   她說有一次她穿了一件很酷的名牌緊身運動褲。

   字彙輔助　1 wear 穿
   　　　　　2 really 真正地
   　　　　　3 cool 酷的
   　　　　　4 brand-named 名牌的
   　　　　　5 workout leggings 緊身運動褲

3. She's a pretty girl, so she didn't think it was so strange when she caught some people staring at her in class.

她是位漂亮女孩，所以當她看到班上有人盯著她看的時候她並不覺得很奇怪。

字彙輔助　　1 pretty 漂亮的

　　　　　　2 think 認為

　　　　　　3 strange 奇怪的

　　　　　　4 stare 盯著

　　　　　　5 class 班級

4. However, it was not until a girl that was late for the class came to the spot in front her did she realize that the girl was wearing the same pair of leggings as her.

但是，一直到有另外一個女生上課遲到，然後那個女生選了在她前面的位置，她才發現那女生跟她穿的是同一條緊身褲。

字彙輔助　　1 late 遲到

　　　　　　2 spot 位置

　　　　　　3 realize 了解

　　　　　　4 the same pair 同一條

　　　　　　5 leggings 緊身褲

▶▶ 字彙、慣用語補充包

字彙、慣用語	中譯
from time to time	有時候
go far	有成就、有作為的
fool around	胡鬧
jam	即興演奏
have my doubts	有我的疑慮

▶▶ 一氣呵成

Q20: What is your most embarrassing yoga moment? 🎧 MP3 66

你做瑜珈最尷尬的時刻是什麼時候？

Oh, I don't personally remember one, but I can tell you a story from a friend of mine. So she said she was wearing these really cool and brand-named workout leggings. She's a pretty girl, so she didn't think it was so strange when she caught some people staring at her in class.

However, it was not until a girl that was late for the class came to the spot in front her did she realize that the girl was wearing the same pair of leggings as her. Those who see through when they were stretched out. You can only imagine how embarrassed I was...I meant she was...

喔，我本身是一個都不記得啦，但我可以跟你說我一個朋友的故事。她說有一次她穿了一件很酷的名牌緊身運動褲。她是位漂亮女孩，所以當她看到班上有人盯著她看的時候並不覺得很奇怪。

但是，一直到有另外一個女生上課遲到，然後那個女生選了在她前面的位置，她發現那女生跟她穿的是同一條

緊身褲。然後她才發現那條緊身褲撐開之後就會變成半透明的。你可以想像我那時候有多尷尬嗎……我是説她有多尷尬啦……

▶▶ 你來試試看

Oh, I don't personally remember one, but I can tell you a story from a friend of mine. _____
_____. _____
_____
_____.

　　However, _____. _____
_____. _____
_____

喔，我本身是一個都不記得啦，但我可以跟你説我一個朋友的故事。_____。
_____。

但是，_____
_____。_____
_____。_____
_____。

口說『演練+實戰』

UNIT 21 ▶▶ 運動

▶▶ 單句口說

1. I went on a road trip in California. It was during the time of the NBA playoffs.

   我到加州公路旅行，那個時候正好是 NBA 季後賽的時候。

   字彙輔助　1 road 路
   　　　　　　2 trip 旅行
   　　　　　　3 California 加州
   　　　　　　4 during 期間
   　　　　　　5 playoff 季後賽

2. we couldn't pass the game in Los Angeles when the Lakers are playing against the Miami Heats.

   所以我們不想錯過湖人隊在洛杉磯跟邁阿密熱火隊的賽事。

   字彙輔助　1 pass 錯過
   　　　　　　2 Los Angeles 洛杉磯
   　　　　　　3 Lakers 湖人隊
   　　　　　　4 play 比賽
   　　　　　　5 Miami Heats 阿密熱火隊

3. It was quite an exciting game to watch.

觀看那場比賽真的很刺激。

字彙輔助　1 quite 相當
　　　　　2 exciting 感到興奮的
　　　　　3 game 遊戲
　　　　　4 watch 觀看

4. You can't beat live NBA playoffs. It was totally worth the drive.

現場觀賞的 NBA 季後賽真的超棒的。完全值得我們開那麼遠的車去看。

字彙輔助　1 beat 擊敗
　　　　　2 live 現場
　　　　　3 playoffs 季後賽
　　　　　4 totally 全然地
　　　　　5 worth 值得

▶▶ 字彙、慣用語補充包

字彙、慣用語	中譯
here and there	到處
believe it or not	信不信由你
food fight	食物大戰
What a relief	真是令人鬆一口氣
keep a safe distance	保持適當距離

▶▶ 一氣呵成

Q21: Have you been to any sports game? How was it? 🎧 MP3 67

你有去看過任何運動的比賽嗎？好玩嗎？

I went on a road trip in California. It was during the time of the NBA playoffs,so we couldn't pass the game in Los Angeles when the Lakers are playing against the Miami Heats.

It was quite an exciting game to watch. You can't beat live NBA playoffs. It was totally worth the drive.

　　我到加州公路旅行，那個時候正好是 NBA 季後賽的時候，所以我們不想錯過在加州的湖人隊在洛杉磯跟邁阿密熱火隊的賽事。

　　那場比賽真的很刺激，而且你真的無法超越現場的 NBA 季後賽。完全值得我們開那麼遠的車去看。

▶▶ 你來試試看

I went on a road trip in California. It was during the time of the NBA playoffs, _____

_____ .

It was quite an exciting game to watch. _____

_____

_____ .

我到加州公路旅行，那個時候正好是 NBA 季後賽的時候，

_____

_____。那場比賽真的很刺激，_____

_____ 。 _____

_____ 。

UNIT 22 ▶▶ Sports 運動

▶▶ 單句口說

1. I've always wanted to try horseback riding.

   我一直以來都很想學騎馬。

   字彙輔助 **1** always 總是

   　　　　　 2 want 想要

   　　　　　 3 try 嘗試

   　　　　　 4 horseback riding 騎馬

2. What's not to love about horses?

   怎麼有可能不喜愛馬？

   字彙輔助 **1** love 喜愛

   　　　　　 2 horse 馬

3. I loved riding the ponies ever since I was a child, but there's a fine line between reality and fantasy.

   我從小就很喜歡騎小馬，但是現實跟幻想之間是有差距的。

   字彙輔助 **1** riding 騎乘

   　　　　　 2 pony 小馬

   　　　　　 3 child 小孩

   　　　　　 4 reality 現實

   　　　　　 5 fantasy 幻想

4. There were several times when I finally decided to do it, I chickened out the second I went on the horseback.

有好幾次我終於決定要去學，可是一騎上馬背我就退縮了。

字彙輔助　🔟 several 好幾個

🔟 finally 終於

🔟 decide 決定

🔟 chicken out 退縮了

🔟 horseback 馬背

▶▶ 字彙、慣用語補充包

字彙、慣用語	中譯
I'm all about it	我最喜歡……、全心投入……
been there and done that	我也經歷過、…已經沒什麼新鮮感了
cried her heart out	哭得十分傷心
big	很紅的
give it a shot	試試看

▶▶ 一氣呵成

Q22: What sport do you want to learn? Why?

🎧 MP3 68

你有想要學什麼運動嗎？為什麼？

I've always wanted to try horseback riding. What's not to love about horses? I loved riding the ponies ever since I was a child, but there's a fine line between reality and fantasy.

There were several times when I finally decided to do it, I chickened out the second I went on the horseback. Oh well...

我一直以來都很想學騎馬。怎麼有可能不喜愛馬？我從小就很喜歡騎小馬，但是現實跟幻想之間是有差距的。

有好幾次我終於決定要去學，可是一騎上馬背我就退縮了。就是這樣囉……

▶▶▶ 你來試試看

I've always wanted to try horseback riding. ＿＿＿＿＿＿
＿＿＿＿＿＿＿＿？ ＿＿＿＿＿＿＿＿＿＿＿＿, but＿
＿＿＿＿＿＿＿＿＿＿＿＿＿＿＿＿＿＿＿.

There were several times when I finally decided to do it.
＿＿＿＿＿＿＿＿＿＿＿＿＿＿＿＿＿＿＿＿
＿＿＿＿＿＿＿＿.

　　我一直以來都很想學騎馬。＿＿＿＿＿＿＿＿？
我＿＿＿＿＿＿＿＿＿＿＿＿＿＿，
但是＿＿＿＿＿＿＿＿＿＿＿＿＿＿＿＿
＿＿＿＿＿＿＿＿。

　　有好幾次我終於決定要去學，＿＿＿＿＿＿＿＿
＿＿＿＿＿＿＿。

口說『演練+實戰』

UNIT 23 ▶▶ 水上活動

▶▶ 單句口說

1. I love going diving when I'm troubled with life.

   每次我生活中遇到難題的時候我就會去潛水。

   字彙輔助　① love 喜愛
   　　　　　② diving 潛水
   　　　　　③ when 當
   　　　　　④ trouble 使煩惱、使憂慮
   　　　　　⑤ life 生活

2. Every single noise just instantly goes away once I'm in the water.

   每次一下水，所有雜音都會立刻消失。

   字彙輔助　① every 每一
   　　　　　② single 單一
   　　　　　③ noise 雜音
   　　　　　④ instantly 立即地
   　　　　　⑤ go away 消失

3. I can only hear my breath and the bubbles I created from the oxygen tank.

我只聽得到我呼吸的聲音和從氧氣筒呼吸時製造的泡泡聲。

字彙輔助　　1 hear 聽到
　　　　　　　2 breath 呼吸
　　　　　　　3 bubble 泡泡
　　　　　　　4 create 創造
　　　　　　　5 oxygen 氧氣

4. It's a really relaxing and peaceful feeling down there.

在水裡真的是很放鬆又很平靜的感覺。

字彙輔助　　1 really 真正地
　　　　　　　2 relaxing 令人感到放鬆的
　　　　　　　3 peaceful 和平的
　　　　　　　4 feel 感覺
　　　　　　　5 down 在下面

▶▶ 字彙、慣用語補充包

字彙、慣用語	中譯
pep talk	精神喊話、鼓勵
you've got to start somewhere	總是得從哪裡開始
pull it off	成功完成、成功做到
flash mob	快閃族
standup comedies	喜劇表演

聽力『講解』

聽力『演練』

聽力『實戰』

口說『演練＋實戰』

▶▶ 一氣呵成

Q23: What is your favorite water sport? Why?

🎧 MP3 69

你最喜歡的水上活動是什麼？為什麼呢？

My favorite water sport is diving. I love going diving when I'm troubled with life. Every single noise just instantly goes away once I'm in the water.

I can only hear my breath and the bubbles I created from the oxygen tank. It's a really relaxing and peaceful feeling down there.

我最喜歡的水上活動是潛水。每次我生活中遇到難題的時候，我就會去潛水。每次一下水，所有雜音都會立刻消失。

我只聽得到我呼吸的聲音和從氧氣筒呼吸時製造的泡泡聲。在水裡真的是很放鬆又很平靜的感覺。

▶▶ 你來試試看

My favorite water sport is diving. _____

_____. _____.

I can only hear my breath and the bubbles I created from the oxygen tank. It's a really relaxing and peaceful feeling down there.

　　我最喜歡的水上活動是潛水。_____

_____。_____

_____。

　　我只聽得到我呼吸的聲音和從氧氣筒呼吸時製造的泡泡聲。在水裡真的是很放鬆又很平靜的感覺。

UNIT 24 ▶▶ Water Sports 水上活動

▶▶ **單句口說**

1. Scariest one was when I stood up paddling with some of my girlfriends in Panama right in front of our resort.

   最恐怖的就是，我跟一些女生朋友們在巴拿馬度假飯店前站立式划槳的時候。

   字彙輔助 1 scariest 最恐怖的
   2 paddling 划槳
   3 girlfriend 女生朋友
   4 Panama 巴拿馬
   5 resort 度假飯店

2. We were just enjoying ourselves out there when one of my friends screamed out "sharks!!" and pointed to the fins on the surface of the water.

   當我們正玩得很開心的時候，其中一個朋友突然尖叫：鯊魚！然後指著水面上的鰭。

   字彙輔助 1 enjoy 享受
   2 friend 朋友
   3 scream out 尖叫
   4 shark 鯊魚
   5 fin 鰭

3. We all screamed together and tried to paddle away from it.

我們一起尖叫，然後試圖划離開那些鰭。

字彙輔助　①　all 所有的

②　scream 尖叫

③　try 試著

④　together 一起

⑤　paddle away 划離

4. We ended up paddling to a school of dolphins.

結果我們最後划到遇到一群海豚。

字彙輔助　①　end up 最後

②　paddling 划槳

③　a school of 一群

④　dolphin 海豚

▶▶ 字彙、慣用語補充包

字彙、慣用語	中譯
one of a kind	獨一無二的
holds a very special place in her heart	在某人的心中有很特別的位置
a dream come true	夢想成真
hands down	無疑的
in tears	含淚

▶▶ 一氣呵成

Q24: What is the scariest experience you had with water sports? 🎧 MP3 70

你有過最恐怖的水上活動的經驗是什麼？

Scariest one was when I stood up paddling with some of my girlfriends in Panama right in front of our resort. We were just enjoying ourselves out there when one of my friends screamed out "sharks!!" and pointed to the fins on the surface of the water.

We all screamed together and tried to paddle away from it. We ended up paddling to a school of dolphins. It was truly a blessing in disguise.

最恐怖的就是，我跟一些女生朋友們在巴拿馬度假飯店前站立式划槳的時候。當我們正玩得很開心的時候，其中一個朋友突然尖叫：鯊魚！然後指著水面上的鰭。

我們一起尖叫，然後試圖划離開那些鰭。結果我們最後划到遇到一群海豚。那真的是因禍得福。

▶▶ 你來試試看

Scariest one was _____.
We were just enjoying ourselves out there when one of my
friends screamed out _____and pointed to
_____.

We all screamed together and _____
_____. _____. It was truly a blessing in
disguise.

　　最恐怖的就是_____
_____。當我們正在玩得開心的時候，其中一個朋友
突然尖叫：_____！然後指著_____
_____。

　　我們一起尖叫，_____。
_____。
那真的是因禍得福。

UNIT 25 ▶▶ 音樂

▶▶ 單句口說

1. I'm gonna go with Reggae. I've been traveling in a lot of islands,

我應該會選雷鬼樂。我已經在很多的島嶼旅行過了。

字彙輔助　❶ go with 與……相配、會選
　　　　　❷ Reggae 雷鬼樂
　　　　　❸ travel 旅行
　　　　　❹ a lot of 很多
　　　　　❺ island 島嶼

2. and they start to grow on me one day, and before I know it, I'm humming the reggae tunes all day.

突然有一天我漸漸開始喜歡雷鬼樂，然後在我反應過來之前，我已經整天都在哼雷鬼的調子了。

字彙輔助　❶ start 開始
　　　　　❷ grow on 對……有越來越大的影響
　　　　　❸ know 知道
　　　　　❹ humming 哼
　　　　　❺ reggae tunes 雷鬼的調子

3. It's a very relaxing, beach music really.

那是一種很令人放鬆，海邊的那種音樂。

字彙輔助
1 very 非常
2 relaxing 令人放鬆的
3 beach 海灘
4 music 音樂
5 really 真正地

4. I'm not too big of a dancer, either, but I can do the swing with Reggae music.

我也不是很會跳舞，但是我可以跟著雷鬼樂搖擺。

字彙輔助
1 big 大的
2 dancer 舞者
3 either 也不（用於否定句）
4 swing 搖擺
5 Reggae music 雷鬼樂

▶▶ 字彙、慣用語補充包

字彙、慣用語	中譯
crime scene	犯罪現場
scarred	對……從此有陰影
in the mood	有心情……想……
see it yourself	親眼看到、親自試試看
killjoy……	掃興的人、煞風景

▶▶ 一氣呵成

Q25: What is your favorite type of music? 🎧 MP3 71
你最喜歡的是哪一類的音樂呢？

I'm gonna go with Reggae. I've been traveling in a lot of islands, and they start to grow on me one day, and before I know it, I'm humming the reggae tunes all day.

It's a very relaxing, beach music really. I'm not too big of a dancer, either, but I can do the swing with Reggae music.

我應該會選雷鬼樂。我已經在很多的島嶼旅行過了，突然有一天我漸漸開始喜歡雷鬼樂，然後在我反應過來之前，我已經整天都在哼雷鬼的調子了。

那是一種很令人放鬆，海邊的那種音樂。我也不是很會跳舞，但是我可以跟著雷鬼樂搖擺。

▶▶ 你來試試看

I'm gonna go with _____. I've been traveling in a lot of islands, and they start to grow on me one day, and before I know it, I'm humming _____ all day.

_____

_____

我應該是會選_____。我已經在很多的島嶼旅行過了。突然有一天我漸漸開始喜歡雷鬼樂，然後在我反應過來之前，我已經整天都在哼_____的調子了。

_____

_____。_____

_____。

UNIT 26 ▶▶ 音樂

▶▶ 單句口說

1. I was visiting some friends in Bogota, Colombia, and one night we went to this tiny bar where there was a singer singing some Latin love songs in the bar.

   我在哥倫比亞的波哥大拜訪朋友的時候，有一天晚上，我們去一個很小的酒吧，台上有一個歌手正在唱著拉丁的情歌。

   字彙輔助　**1** visit
   　　　　　2 Bogota 波哥大
   　　　　　3 Colombia 哥倫比亞
   　　　　　4 tiny 很小的
   　　　　　5 singer 歌手

2. Everything looked very normal until the singer walked to my friends, and asked them in Spanish what kind of music I like, I told him Reggaeton, which is like the Spanish version of Hip-Pop I really like back then.

   一切看起來都很正常，直到那個歌手走向我的朋友並用西班牙文問他們我喜歡哪一種音樂，我跟他說雷鬼動，也就是我以前很喜歡的很像是西文版的嘻哈音樂。

   字彙輔助　**1** normal 普通的
   　　　　　2 singer 歌手
   　　　　　3 Spanish 西班牙文

4 version 版本

3. He walked back and talked to other musicians, and then he started to sing my favorite Reggaeton song.

他走回去樂團跟其他樂手說話，然後他就開始唱我最喜歡的雷鬼動的歌。

字彙輔助　　1 walk 行走

2 talk 說話

3 musician 樂手

4 start 開始

5 sing 唱歌

4. The whole bar started to dance, and he came singing to me and danced with me!

整個酒吧都在跳舞，他還來對我唱歌和跟我一起跳舞。

字彙輔助　　1 whole 整個

2 dance 跳舞

▶▶ 字彙、慣用語補充包

字彙、慣用語	中譯
push it	得寸進尺
is born to……	生下來做……
couldn't pass that concert up	不能放棄……
It depends	看情況
go downhill	走下坡

▶▶ 一氣呵成

Q26: What's the most unique experience you have related to music? 🎧 MP3 72

你有關於音樂最獨特的經驗嗎？

I was visiting some friends in Bogota, Colombia, and one night we went to this tiny bar where there was a singer singing some Latin love songs in the bar. Everything looked very normal until the singer walked to my friends, and asked them in Spanish what kind of music I like, I told him Reggaeton, which is like the Spanish version of Hip-Pop I really like back then.

He walked back and started talking to other musicians, and then he started to sing my favorite Reggaeton song. The whole bar started to dance, and he came singing to me and danced with me!

我在哥倫比亞的波哥大拜訪朋友的時候，有一天晚上，我們去一個很小的酒吧，台上有一個歌手正在唱著拉丁的情歌。一切看起來都很正常，直到那個歌手走向我的朋友並用西班牙文問他們我喜歡哪一種音樂，我跟他說雷鬼動，也就是我以前很喜歡的很像是西文版的嘻哈音樂。

他走回去樂團跟其他樂手說話，然後他就開始唱我最喜歡的雷鬼動的歌。整個酒吧都在跳舞，他還來對我唱歌和跟我一起跳舞。

▶▶ 你來試試看

I was visiting some friends in _____ and one night we went to this tiny bar where there was a singer singing some Latin love songs in the bar. _____

_____

_____

_____.

_____

_____

_____.

　　我在_____拜訪朋友的時候，有一天晚上我們去一個很小的酒吧，台上有一個歌手正在唱著拉丁的情歌。_____

_____

_____

_____。

_____

_____。_____

_____。

UNIT 27 ▶▶ Festivals 節日慶典

▶▶ **單句口說**

1. I went to the Carnival of Venice and it was such a gorgeous festival.

   我去了威尼斯的嘉年華會。那個節慶真是超美的。

   字彙輔助 ❶ Carnival 嘉年華會
   ❷ Venice 威尼斯
   ❸ such 如此的
   ❹ gorgeous 美麗的
   ❺ festival 節慶

2. Everyone dressed up nicely and wore these amazing masks.

   大家都精心打扮，然後還戴了很棒的面具。

   字彙輔助 ❶ everyone 每個人
   ❷ dressed up 盛裝打扮
   ❸ nicely 漂亮地、出色地
   ❹ wear 穿、戴
   ❺ mask 面具

3. I had to buy so many of those masks before I left Venice.

我在離開威尼斯之前不得不買很多面具。

字彙輔助　❶ buy 買

　　　　❷ many 許多

　　　　❸ those 那些

　　　　❹ before 之前

4. There were fireworks by the canal, too.

在運河旁也有放煙火。

字彙輔助　❶ there were 有

　　　　❷ fireworks 煙火

　　　　❸ canal 運河

　　　　❹ too 也

▶▶ 字彙、慣用語補充包

字彙、慣用語	中譯
I can see that happen	我覺得很有可能
totally	當然
people watching	觀察周遭的人
get the hang of it	抓到訣竅
get a sense of	體驗一下當……的感覺、感覺一下…

聽力『講解』

聽力『演練』

聽力『實戰』

口說『演練＋實戰』

▶▶ 一氣呵成

Q27: What is the most impressive festival you have ever been to? 🎧 MP3 73

你去過最令你印象深刻的節慶是什麼？

I went to the Carnival of Venice and it was such a gorgeous festival. Everyone dressed up nicely and wore these amazing masks. I had to buy so many of those masks before I left Venice.

There were fireworks by the canal, too. Very impressive and when can you dress up like that with so many people anyways?

我去了威尼斯的嘉年華會。那個節慶真是超美的。大家都精心打扮，然後還，戴了很棒的面具。我在離開威尼斯之前不得不買很多面具。

在運河旁也有放煙火。超令人印象深刻的，而且你還可以去哪裡精心打扮成那樣？

▶▶ 你來試試看

I went to _____
_____. Everyone dressed up nicely and wore these
amazing masks. _____
_____.

There were fireworks by the canal, too. _____
_____
_____?

我去了 _____
_____。大家都精心打扮，然後還帶了很棒的面具。_____
_____
_____。

在運河旁也有放煙火。_____
_____
_____?

UNIT 28 ▶▶ Festivals 節日慶典

▶▶ **單句口說**

1. The strangest festival I've heard of is the Day of the Dead that's celebrated in Mexico.

   我聽過最奇怪的節慶是墨西哥的亡靈節。

   字彙輔助 1 strangest 最奇怪的

   2 festival 節慶

   3 hear 聽說

   4 the Day of the Dead 亡靈節

   5 celebrate 慶祝

2. At the beginning, it's strange for me that people "celebrate" the fact that their family is dead, but then I thought that is such a good idea.

   一開始的時候我覺得很奇怪,為什麼他們要「慶祝」亡靈,可是我後來覺得這真的是蠻好的點子。

   字彙輔助 1 beginning 開始

   2 strange 奇怪的

   3 family 家庭

   4 such 如此的

   5 good 好的

3. On this day, the families gather together, have fun and share stories about their family that had passed away.

在這天，家人會聚在一起玩樂，和互相分享死去家人的故事。

字彙輔助　　1 gather 團聚

2 together 一起

3 fun 樂趣

4 share 分享

5 pass away 過世

4. A strange but good idea!

很奇怪，但是是個好主意。

字彙輔助　　1 idea 想法

▶▶ 字彙、慣用語補充包

字彙、慣用語	中譯
talent show	才藝表演
rock	把……做得很好、把……穿得很好看
mix and match	混搭
go back in time	時光倒流、回到過去
makeover	改裝

▶▶ 一氣呵成

Q28: What is the strangest festival you have ever heard of? 🎧 MP3 74

你聽過最奇怪的節慶是什麼呢？

The strangest festival I've heard of is the Day of the Dead that's celebrated in Mexico. At the beginning, it's strange for me that people "celebrate" the fact that their family is dead, but then I thought that this is such a good idea.

On this day, the families gather together, have fun and share stories about their family that had passed away. A strange but good idea!

我聽過最奇怪的節慶是墨西哥的亡靈節。一開始的時候我覺得很奇怪，為什麼他們要「慶祝」亡靈，可是我後來覺得這真的是蠻好的點子。

在這天，家人會聚在一起玩樂，和互相分享死去家人的故事。很奇怪，但是是個好主意。

▶▶ 你來試試看

The strangest festival I've heard of is _____

_____

_____

_____

_____..

On this day,_____

_____

_____

_____.

　　我聽過最奇怪的節慶是_____

_____

_____.

　　在這天，_____

_____

_____

_____。

UNIT 29 ▶▶ Amusement Park 遊樂園

▶▶ 單句口說

1. I would dedicate my worst experience to the Haunted House at L.A. Universal Studio.

   我要把我在遊樂園最糟的經驗歸咎於洛杉磯環球影城的鬼屋。

   字彙輔助 　**1** dedicate 致力於

   　　　　　 2 worst 最糟的

   　　　　　 3 experience 經驗

   　　　　　 4 Haunted House 鬼屋

   　　　　　 5 Universal Studio 環球影城

2. Their problem was that they took everything way too seriously.

   他們的問題就是他們太認真了啦。

   字彙輔助 　**1** problem 問題

   　　　　　 2 too 太過於

   　　　　　 3 seriously 嚴肅地

3. It was a walking tour through the whole haunted house.

   那是一個要走路穿過整座鬼屋的行程。

   字彙輔助 　**1** walking 行走

2 tour 旅行、旅遊

3 through 穿過

4 whole 整個

4. Everything in the haunted house was as if they came out directly from the crime scene.

鬼屋裡面的所有東西都好像是直接從犯罪現場搬來的。

字彙輔助　　1 everything 每件事

2 come out 從……出來

3 directly 直接地

4 crime 犯罪

5 scene 場景

▶▶ 字彙、慣用語補充包

字彙、慣用語	中譯
is never an easy chore	……從來就不是一件簡單的差事
give it a try	試試看
throw up a little in my mouth	……讓我想吐
foodie	美食家
not the biggest fan of	沒有特別喜歡……

▶▶ 一氣呵成

Q29: What was your worst experience in the amusement park? 🎧 MP3 75

你在遊樂園裡最糟的經驗是什麼？

I would dedicate my worst experience to the Haunted House at L.A. Universal Studio. Their problem was that they took everything way too seriously.

It was a walking tour through the whole haunted house. Everything in the haunted house was as if they came out directly from the crime scene. I had nightmares and was scarred to go to any haunted house after that one.

我要把我在遊樂園最糟的經驗歸咎於洛杉磯環球影城的鬼屋。他們的問題就是他們太認真了啦。

那是一個要走路穿過整座鬼屋的行程。鬼屋裡面的所有東西都好像是直接從犯罪現場搬來的。我在去玩那個鬼屋之後就做惡夢而且也就從此對鬼屋有陰影。

▶▶ 你來試試看

I would dedicate my worst experience to _____
_____._____
_____
_____.

_____
_____
_____._____
_____.

我要把我在遊樂園最糟的經驗歸咎於_____
__。_____。

_____
_____
_____。

UNIT 30 ▶▶ Amusement Park 遊樂園

▶▶ 單句口說

1. I've been to almost all the Disneyland in the world, and I can't say I like any particular one.

   我幾乎去遍全世界所有的迪士尼樂園，但是我說不出來我最喜歡哪一個。

   字彙輔助　1 almost 幾乎
   　　　　　2 all 所有的
   　　　　　3 Disneyland 迪士尼樂園
   　　　　　4 like 喜歡
   　　　　　5 particular 特別的

2. They are all unique in their own ways.

   它們都有自己獨特的地方。

   字彙輔助　1 unique 獨特的
   　　　　　2 in their own ways 有自己的方式

3. Cinderella's castle, the carousel, and all the magic in the park.

   仙杜瑞拉的城堡、旋轉木馬還有園內所有的魔法。

   字彙輔助　1 Cinderella 仙杜瑞拉、灰姑娘
   　　　　　2 castle 城堡

　　③ carousel 旋轉木馬

　　④ magic 魔術

　　⑤ park 公園

4. It feels like a dream come true when I'm in Disney-land.

在迪士尼樂園裡就好像是夢想成真一樣！

字彙輔助　① feels like 感覺好似、想要

　　　　② dream 夢想

　　　　③ come true 實現

　　　　④ when 當

▶▶ 字彙、慣用語補充包

字彙、慣用語	中譯
It's just not quite the same	感覺就是不太一樣
hooked	上癮
for the sake of	看在……的份上
an icing on the cake	好上加好、錦上添花
pair with	配對

▶▶ 一氣呵成

Q30: What is your favorite amusement park?

🎧 MP3 76

你最喜歡哪一間遊樂園？

Disneyland!! It is just the best amusement ever. I've been to almost all the Disneyland in the world, and I can't say I like any particular one.

They are all unique in their own ways. Who doesn't like Disneyland really? Cinderella's castle, the carousel, and all the magic in the park. It feels like a dream come true when I'm in Disneyland.

迪士尼樂園！它就是有史以來最棒的遊樂園啊！我幾乎去遍全世界所有的迪士尼樂園，但是我說不出來我最喜歡哪一個。

它們都有自己獨特的地方。不過說真的怎麼可能會有人不喜歡迪士尼樂園？仙杜瑞拉的城堡、旋轉木馬還有園內所有的魔法。在迪士尼樂園裡就好像是夢想成真一樣！

▶▶ **你來試試看**

_____

_____

_____

_____.

They are all unique in their own ways. _____

_____

_____

_____

_____.

_____

_____

_____.

它們都有自己獨特的地方。_____

_____

_____

_____.

考用英語系列 001

一次就考到雅思說、聽 6.5+（附 MP3）

作　　者　倍斯特編輯部
發 行 人　周瑞德
執行總監　齊心瑀
行銷經理　楊景輝
企劃編輯　陳韋佑
封面構成　高鍾琪

內頁構成　菩薩蠻數位文化有限公司
印　　製　大亞彩色印刷製版股份有限公司
初　　版　2017 年 6 月
定　　價　新台幣 399 元
出　　版　倍斯特出版事業有限公司
電　　話　(02) 2351-2007
傳　　真　(02) 2351-0887
地　　址　100 台北市中正區福州街 1 號 10 樓之 2
E - m a i l　best.books.service@gmail.com
網　　址　www.bestbookstw.com

港澳地區總經銷　泛華發行代理有限公司
地　　　　址　香港新界將軍澳工業邨駿昌街 7 號 2 樓
電　　　　話　(852) 2798-2323
傳　　　　真　(852) 2796-5471

國家圖書館出版品預行編目(CIP)資料

一次就考到雅思說、聽 6.5+ / 倍斯特編輯
部著. -- 初版. -- 臺北市 ： 倍斯特,
2017.06 面 ； 　 公分. --（考用英語系列 ；
1）ISBN 978-986-94428-6-2（平裝附光碟片）

1.國際英語語文測試系統 2.考試指南

　805.189　　　　　　　106006683